Gut

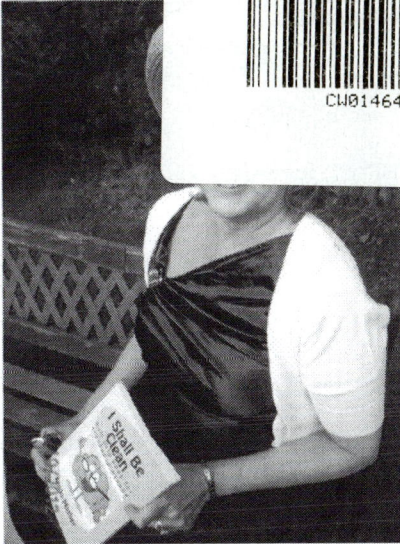

Linda was born in Easington Colliery, Co Durham in 1958, and then moved to Leicester in the early 1960's, which is where she spent her childhood. But, it was in 'Shakespeare County,' Warwickshire, where she says she 'grew up' during and after completing her counselling diploma.

She is now an experienced counsellor, supervisor, & trainer, behavioral family therapist & author of self help books. She has three grown up children and eight grandchildren.

This is Linda's first novel.

Gut Instinct

Also by Linda Mather

Self help books:

I shall wear purple

I shall be blue

I shall be clean

Gut instinct is Linda's first novel

Gut Instinct

Gut Instinct

Linda Mather

GUT

INSTINCT

Gut Instinct

Gut Instinct

For my Auntie Anne Theobald, who would have loved this book, and was the loveliest woman and kindest of friends. She is missed by all that loved her and knew her.

Forever in our hearts.

****

For my Grandma Violet Burns who adored me as much as my mum did and greatly encouraged my creativity.

Forever in our hearts

****

For my Dad Owen Williams who would have been so proud. Life will never be the same without you; singing solo is not the same.

Forever in our hearts

To

Chris

Best Wishes

Linda Mathew.

"A man who has been the undisputable favourite
of his mother keeps for life the feeling of a
conqueror" – Sigmund Freud

<u>Prologue</u>

"I knew I was an unwanted baby when I saw my bath toys were a toaster and a radio"

I've never forgotten that quote,

I'd read it in one of my mothers magazines, it was Joan Rivers and I had spent hours admiring her photograph believing that this was what I should look like, be like.

I was about thirteen at the time. She, Joan Rivers, had the same kind of mother as I had. I no longer felt so alone in the world, knowing there were others just like me.

One day I will be famous I had thought, and I will say things like that, let them know exactly what my mother was – a whore, a child abuser and a nonentity, at least she was now.

I'd had dreams, dreams that never came true, my life, and my waking hours had been one long nightmare and my sleep had been my respite where I could wish for happier times, when I could dream about blissful times, about becoming someone like Joan Rivers.

My dreams are what kept me sane, kept me from wanting to die, when I awoke from the dream I would want to sleep again to go back into the dream that helped me to escape my miserable life.

Being born is like a lottery, you don't know which mother you are going to get. I was number 326 lining up waiting to be embedded in some woman's womb; ironically 325 didn't feel well on the day of my consummation so was made to sit out.

If he had been well then my life might have been so very different, I would have got a nice mother then. Instead I got 'her'; instead I drew the short straw.

Did your child get the short straw?

Hey you! I'm talking to you!

Put the book down,

YES YOU!

Did your child get the short straw or was he lucky and won the lottery!

"We are not makers of history. We are made by history" – Martin Luther King Junior

This means that I have been made by my history, my life has made me who I am and also my mother, she has made me who I am today.

Or would I have been like this anyway, was it in my DNA, was it nature or nurture?

Perhaps you will be able to answer my question after reading my story, after living in my world even if just for the time it takes to read this book, or after stepping into the shoes that I was forced to wear either by my upbringing or by my DNA.

So please don't judge me as you read my story as this could have been you, if you had drawn the short straw like I did.

****

<u>Chapter One</u>

Saturday 8th March

The call had come in at twelve fifteen and Detective Sergeant Stephen Roberts was sitting at his desk going through all the papers that had been prepared for the Crime Prosecution Service for a rape case, that they had been working on.

It was not unusual for him to be in his office on a Saturday morning, he used this time when the station was quiet to do paperwork. They never seemed to have the time in the week.

Unlike most other professions, in the police force they were never allocated with paperwork time. Merely, had to do it when they could and Saturday mornings were the only time Stephen found that he could. You couldn't turn down jobs because you had paperwork to do, if you were called out that was it, everything else had to go on hold.

He was the only one in, and it was extremely quiet, ghostly quiet in fact, most of his staff had the weekend off, there had been nothing urgent brewing, he was the head of the homicide division and thankfully murders didn't occur every week.

He was feeling relatively pleased with his team, they'd cleared this case up pretty quickly. They had speedily and smoothly arrested and charged a twenty five year old lad who had raped and killed a girl under the influence of methamphetamine, he was now safely tucked up in a cell in Leicester prison, remanded until his appearance in court.

All that was left to do was ensure that they presented an airtight case against him, and as was customary the CPS relied on them to do that.

Stephen was a handsome man for fifty two, almost six foot and had a physique akin to someone who was a frequent visitor to the gym. He wasn't. He had only ever been to the gym once in his life, he was just lucky to have genes that maintained this muscular build.

He had dark hair with distinguished grey streaks and presented in a confident but not arrogant manner. His most striking feature were his eyes, they were a deep blue with long dark lashes serenading them, eyes that you could imagine falling into, and find yourself swimming in a warm pool of clear blue water.

He had been a detective sergeant for four years now and thoroughly enjoyed his job. He prided himself on being a fair boss, a good cop and was well and truly respected by his team, and his management.

The paperwork was almost done and he was about to wrap up, go home and preen himself for his night in with Tanya, his girlfriend, when his mobile vibrated and then rang on his desk, it was the standard ring tone that came with the phone.

Stephen hated the song tunes that incessantly boomed out in the station when it was busy. He had put forward a suggestion to have them banned as he felt that they were a distraction, he had wanted everyone to have the standard ring tones, but it hadn't gone down very well. So he'd binned that idea for the time being and hoped that people would follow his example.

"Stephen Roberts" he'd answered, and listened patiently to the caller on the other end.

The next thing he knew he was in his car and reversing out of the station car park, with all thoughts of this rape case and telephone ring tones out of his mind.

There was something much more serious for him to deal with now.

The traffic was mild today on the streets of Leicester possibly because of the gentle rain that was coming down, rain that hadn't stopped all day. In fact for the last few months it had rained most days "wouldn't stop a hose pipe ban in the summer though" Stephen had thought, drumming his fingers on the steering wheel to the rhythm of his window wipers.

He sped past the shops, houses and factories without giving them a second glance. He knew where he was heading, he knew the area well.

The Peckleton Estate was a run- down council estate at the other side of town. He'd spent a good majority of his time on this estate as a rookie cop, dealing with a many number of issues from domestic violence to drug dealing.

It was an area that was once a tidy housing estate for those that couldn't afford their own home's, but had now become a neighbourhood of poverty, drug use and juvenile offenders. The resident's proudly collecting asbo's as if they were medals of honour.

He turned into a cul-de-sac and immediately saw the yellow and black police tape already in place blowing softly in the mild breeze, opposite the wasteland.

Behind the tape was an unusual amount of onlookers, curiosity etched on their faces.

He was on Bakewell Road which had a row of council houses on the left hand side and on the right was a working men's club, next to this was a wasteland that had recently boasted a children's play area, which had already been pulled apart and defaced with graffiti.

At club opening times the play area would be full of kids, content with their pop and crisps having been left outside to play whilst their parents were inside drinking themselves to a stupor.

This Stephen thought would account for the crowds of people hovering on the wasteland, he looked at the clock on his dashboard, it was twelve forty five, and a Saturday, and the club would have been packed at this time. It wouldn't have taken long for word to get around.

He pulled up behind two police cars and a forensic van, got out of the car and took a quick glance at the onlookers, some holding pints of beer, nosey, but not nosey enough to leave their drinks on the bar. Kids sitting on their bike's, or with skateboards tucked under their arms.

They were all looking at him, no doubt inquisitively wondering who he was.

Was he someone they could ask what was going on, so that they could spread rumours instantly around their peers, adding bits on, the more gruesome the better enabling them to score points. It was their warped perception of information sharing, so that they could then bask in their own glory. For a while, a very short while at least, their kudos inflated.

He walked up to the house, ducked under the police tape and showed his card to the officer on guard outside the crime scene.

Stephen didn't know what to expect when he entered the house, he'd not been given all the details, he'd not asked for them, he had been too eager to get there and get down to work.

He was pleased to see that two of his officers Derek Angus and John Waterstone had followed all the necessary procedures. The police tape had been put in place and the scene of crime officers were there in their white ghost like overalls protecting the scene, and collecting evidence that would be vital to a court case.

Just as John had come into his thoughts he spotted him walking towards him, looking calm but a shade whiter than he normally looked.

"What's cooking?" he asked, as John approached him.

"Girl dead sir" he replied "Jane Smith, thirty five years old, single mum. Looks like she has been suffocated with her own pillow, she was found this morning by her sister who had been babysitting her little boy, she brought him back at eleven as had been pre-arranged and she found her on the floor dead."

"Any leads? Where are the sister and kid now?" Stephen asked.

"No leads as yet sir, sister's in the kitchen in absolute bits, we've not been able to talk to her yet and the kid is with a neighbour, do you want me to try and talk to her now sir?"

"No, just carry on with what you were doing and I will talk to her after I've spoken to the pathologist, I assume he's here is he?"

"Just arrived before you sir, he's in the living room with the er.. body"

"Any sign of forced entry or anything missing?" Stephen asked almost as an afterthought.

"No sir, to the forced entry, not sure if any things missing till we speak to the sister, but nothing obvious"

"Okay John thank you for your good work, we'll catch up later" he said as he walked away in the direction of the living room.

He was pleased that it was not going to be too gory a scene, but thinking that it was an unusual cause of death, he couldn't recall being called out to a death by suffocation before, not by a pillow anyway.

Chapter Two

Stephen sat at his desk at the station, looking at the evidence before him; he had called a meeting for the following morning with his team to look at what had been done so far in the investigation and what they needed to do.

He'd sent Derek and John on a door to door with immediate neighbours this evening and to try and track down and speak to the friends that she was out with.

There was not a lot they could do until they got the pathologist report in, but he knew that he would find something, there would be no weekend leave this weekend and those that were off had been called in. He needed his full team to put this one to bed.

He thought about all the onlookers at the scene, the people watching curiosity etched on their faces, his mind's eye thinking back to those faces. Anyone of them could have been the killer, come back to look at his handy work or to get off on what he had done.

He made a note to himself to look through the notes or statements that he had asked the uniform guys to get from the bystanders if they had seen anything.

Stephen had spoken to the pathologist on the scene and he had said that she had most certainly been suffocated and that the time of death would have been approximately between the hours of 2 a.m and 4 a.m.

He had said that he wouldn't know if there had been any sexual assault until he got her to the lab, but there were no external bruising which sometimes can indicate that type of attack, but he was not ruling it out. He'd assured Stephen that he would report in as soon as he had anything.

Stephen had also spoken to the sister; she was extremely upset, but didn't know much at all.

Jane was a single parent of a 4 year old boy and that she had babysat for her most Friday nights while she went out with the girls.

The father of the child was a builder, he worked abroad most of the time and that he was currently in Germany. She believed that he was expected back in about a week's time for a week's holiday and he had planned to spend that time with his son.

Although Jane and her ex had encountered a volatile relationship at the time they were together, they had an amicable relationship now for the sake of the boy.

Jane hadn't been in any other relationship as far as she knew and was not involved in anything that could have put her in danger.

There was nothing much to go on there then, he reflected, nothing much at all.

It was a mystery, Stephen thought, not something he had ever come across before.

He picked up the polythene evidence bag and stared at the contents for a long time.

A small white card one inch by three inches, it had been cut to size around two sides. This was the strangest piece of evidence they had, the only piece of evidence they had at the moment, the writing on it typed in bold capital letters in what looked like times new roman. It had been found in her hand:

GUESS WHO?

Who was that message for he wondered, there was something not quite right about this, it wasn't a spontaneous murder, and it was definitely pre-meditated, if the perpetrator had gone to the trouble of making this card.

Someone wanted someone to know that he had done this.

Who and why?

Why would anyone suffocate a girl and then leave a card saying this. Perhaps it was a message for the estranged husband, perhaps he had upset someone and this was his payback.

Or the sister, although she didn't look as though she was hiding anything, she seemed pretty sincere and Stephen was quite good at picking up signs of people lying.

She gave good eye contact, was not fidgety at all, nor was she sweating or in any great rush to get away, which was often the signs of people who were lying and her story, was very precise.

He picked the phone up and rang Tanya, he had left a message on her answering machine to cancel this evening, but it was still early yet and he was ready to get out of this place and have some fun. Switch off for a while.

He had learned over the years that you could over think and that was dangerous when investigating a case. You could lose sight of the facts or miss something of significance. So sometimes it was more helpful to focus on something else for a while and go back to things with a fresh mind and a fresh eye.

He knew exactly what would do this, a passionate night with Tanya, sex was always something that cleared his mind for a while.

Tanya had been his girlfriend for eight months now and she was beginning to feel like a cosy pair of slippers to him. He didn't mind that, he liked it; he hated the 'newness' of a relationship, he got no joy from the insecurity, the anticipation or the anxieties of the initial dates.

"Hello" her husky voice came on the line.

"Hi honey, did you get my message? He asked endearingly.

"Yes, yes, that's fine, no problem."

"Well I've just finished up here now love and wondered if you fancied some company?" he asked anxiously hoping for an affirmative reply.

"Yes, no problem, I'll put some wine on ice" and she put down the phone before he could reply, knowing that he would be requesting something 'naughty' and not in the mood to play telephone sex games.

He grabbed his coat and headed out of the the station whistling, happy that he was going to get laid.

<u>Chapter Three</u>

Sunday 9th March

It was 8.30 a.m. Sunday morning and Stephen was preparing his notes for the 9.00 a.m meeting he had called with his team.

They'd all arrived, he had seen them wandering in, some were buzzing around with excited anticipation and others were dragging their feet, candidly pissed off with being called in on their day off.

It was just a small team, down to the usual limited resources, a team of eight, but all had come in and that was the main thing, he could cope with their disinclination as long as they had turned in. He sensed that they would need all the man power they had for this one.

He headed to the men's room to smarten his tie, have one last check over that he was looking the part and by 8.50 he was heading for the conference room, now also known as the training room. There was never any training on a Sunday, so he was sure they'd be left alone.

Punctuality was his middle name, he always tried to be on time, he hated it when people were late so tried to practice what he preached.

The room was fuller than he had expected, ten people in total, two beat Bobbies were sat talking to Derek and John. They had probably come to offer their assistance, which was good of them he thought, if they hadn't got the ulterior motive of wanting to join the plain clothes division, but what the hell the more hands on deck, the quicker we will find this asshole and book him.

The room was bustling with conversation all contributing their ideas to the "who dun nit" mystery that was surrounding this case, no doubt. But now was the time for them to share those ideas in an open forum.

Stephen put up his hand to command silence and the whole room stopped talking instantaneously. He loved that, he loved his own authority and the fact that people responded so quickly to his authority. It was one of the reasons he loved his job, that and the money of course.

"Right as is the usual procedure let's look at what we have got up to now, and then we will look at where we are going with this" Stephen said confidently and firmly, everyone listened attentively, as some had only just come on that morning and had only gathered titbits from their colleagues.

"We have a thirty five year old single mother found dead in her home. The victims name was Jane Smith."

A snigger went around the room, amused by the girl's name which is not surprising as it significantly sounded like 'Jane Doe.' Stephen ignored this idiocy and carried on.

"Time of murder is reported to be between the hours of 2 a.m. and 4 a.m." he looked around the room at the now subdued faces of his team, as they realised that he was in no mood for joking about and continued.

"There was no forced entry so that leads us to think that she knew the perpetrator. The girl was suffocated to death with her own pillow and had in her hand a card that said Guess who." He paused for a couple of seconds to let this bit of information register.

"She was found by her sister who was babysitting her child, and she made a call to 999 at around 11.15 a.m.

Jane has an ex partner, the father of the her four year old boy who is currently working in Germany and due back next week, reportedly their relationship although once volatile is now amicable. She has no current boyfriend that her sister is aware of" he ended, that was it that was all he had to offer.

The team sat there, waiting for more, expecting more and he could see their disappointment when they realised he had none and was now finished.

"So, Derek, John what do you have?" he asked.

"Not much more sir I'm afraid" John replied "She'd been to a nightclub, Jason's with two friends, they had a good night, no-one specifically hanging around them or chatting them up, they were just enjoying themselves as girls do.

At the end of the night, they went to a burger van and got something to eat, again nothing unusual happened then the three of them got a taxi, Jane getting out second. That was the last they saw of her" John finished letting Derek take over.

"None of the neighbours knew her too well, she'd only moved in her current home around six months ago" Derek accounted glad to have a piece of the action.

"They stated that she was a quiet girl, didn't really mix, and seemed a good mum to her little boy. No visitors seen going to her house, only her sister and they heard nothing unusual on the night in question"

Again there was an interlude of silence, people waiting to hear more, astonished that there was nothing more, nothing to get their teeth into, not even a nibble of something.

Stephen once more broke the silence, feeling as discouraged as his team felt but trying hard not to show it.

"We are still waiting for the pathologist's report, so hopefully that will give us something more to go on. However, I'm opening the floor now for any suggestions or ideas?"

Silence.

What could anyone say, there was nothing to say, there were no ingredients so how the hell were they to bake the cake, Stephen thought despondently.

He was just about to give people their tasks for the day and end the meeting when he noticed Paul, one of his team members last to join his squad, with his hand half in the air.

"Yes Paul" he said.

"The card sir, it could be a calling card"

"A calling card" he asked.

"Yes this is the m.o. of a serial killer sir, something they always leave at the scene"

Stephen was feeling irritated, this guy rubbed him up the wrong way anyway with his University degree, thinking he knew it all just because he'd done a degree in criminology.

"I'm sorry" he replied aware that all eyes were on him "is there another death that I'm unaware of?"

"Well no..............."

"Then my understanding is that for it to be a serial killer there has to be more than one body, so until there is let's cut with the psychobabble crap, and concentrate on this case.

Police work is NOT about psychobabble it's about getting out on the streets and listening to your gut instinct and working with that. Have I made myself clear?" he asked directing his piercing blue eyes at Paul and not faltering.

"Yes sir" Paul answered visibly struggling to restrain his anger.

"Good I'll be in my office if anyone needs me and Paul"

"Yes"

"Isn't paranoia pending a panic attack!"

The whole room sniggered as Stephen left the office abruptly managing to conceal his own anger at the stupidity of this imbecile that he was forced to have on his team.

Chapter Four

It was late Sunday evening and Paul had just gotten in he was still fuming from the meeting this morning, stomping around the house, banging plates down on his kitchen bar, cursing at the audacity of his boss. His anger had rankled all day and he'd struggled to let it go.

Stephen had deliberately humiliated him in front of his colleagues. Made him look a twat!

Well he hadn't heard the last of that!

"Prick" he shouted out loud,

No-one would hear him as he lived alone. He lived in a rented flat after separating from his girlfriend, it was very basic, but he had all the things that he needed.

His mum would pop round occasionally and tidy the place up as mothers do and then he wouldn't be able to find anything and she'd turn up with something new sometimes and try to make the place look more homely, bloody fluffy cushions or throws or something, but he very rarely brought anything himself, unless it was electronic

Paul had started his career as a trainee electrician; he'd messed around a lot in his youth and looked for trouble, in fact thinking back he was always up to no good.

Mercifully he was clever enough not to get caught. A couple of driving offences was all he had and thankfully they had not affected him getting into the police force.

It was inevitable he would join the police one day he thought. It had been on the cards since he was born when his mother had named him Paul Christian. PC Spencer she'd always said had a nice ring to it; imagine if you joined the police force, you would be PC PC Spencer.

It wasn't his life plan though; he had preferred being on the other side of the law when he was younger, nicking cars, smoking dope and partying every weekend at some rave or another. Downing ecstasy like they were smarties.

He had changed his life around when he was twenty five and gone back to college redone his GCSE's and sat three A' levels with A grades and consequently had been accepted into Coventry University to do a degree in criminology.

It was then that he had decided to join the police, found it a little amusing to be honest, bad boy turned good.

His family had been real proud of him too, glad to see that he was doing something constructive with his life, he must have been a worry he thought, especially to his mum.

She had been a single parent and brought him and his two younger sisters up on her own, she liked to think she'd made a good job of it, and she had. They had fell out when his life went a little wayward, needless to say she didn't know how to handle him, but they were close again and that was important to him.

Look at him now; he'd managed to get into the plain clothes squad pretty quickly making some of his mates jealous. That was the way it worked in the police, you either worked your way up, or took a degree and jumped the queue.

He'd jumped the queue but he hadn't joined the police to be humiliated, not by some wanker that thought he knew it all.

Paul knew that his anger would fester all night if he didn't have a joint, so he got out his stash and began to roll one knowing that this would calm him down, chill him out.

He didn't use any other drugs anymore, just cannabis now and again, well most nights if he was honest, it was one last bit of rebellion he wasn't prepared to give up, not unless they started drug testing at the station, then he'd have no choice. He'd have to stop if he wanted to keep his job.

He never touched alcohol, didn't like it and it would piss him right off if he had to give up his dope whilst the rest of them drank themselves into oblivion at the end of their shift.

He took a long drag on his joint and settled back into the chair, the contents of the drug rushing through his body and rapidly soothing his anger.

He was convinced this was not a one off, no matter what Stephen Roberts said, but maybe he should have perhaps kept his thoughts to himself though, in hindsight he had been a bit premature but they weren't as educated as he was, would never quite 'get it' not like he did.

He'd studied hard at university, knew his stuff, had waited for this day when he could put his skills to good use and that had been thwarted by his boss.

He could understand him being sceptical, jealous even, worried about being undermined, but there was no need to emasculate him in that way, not in front of everyone.

There would be another murder he was confident of it, then that would show them, show them who the clever one was. Then Stephen fucking Roberts would have no choice but to let him do what he was trained to do.

He thought back to the case and what they had so far, what was it that had convinced him that this was not just a one off.

The card, it was a 'calling card' he was sure of that. It made no sense otherwise. Why would someone even bother to leave a card if he didn't want to taunt the police, if he had no plans to do it again?

The joint was kicking in big style now; he felt whoozy, his thoughts starting to converge into one another, no point wallowing over today he thought. They will see in the end, see that he was right all along.

Chapter Five

Stephen was on his way home, it had been another long day and they were no further forward in their investigation. Nothing had come up in the house to house enquiries and despite what Paul (criminal psychology nut) thought his gut told him that this was a one off. His gut was usually always right.

Paul, why did he dislike this man so much, he knew that he had been hard on him today, but he had a knack of getting his back up. Had done since the day he'd been put on his team, new boy just left university and thought he knew more than those on his team that had worked the streets for the same amount of time as he had sat in a comfy classroom learning the ropes from a bloody text book.

A serial killer I ask you. One murder and all of a sudden they've got a serial killer on their hands!

This murder was down to a disgruntled friend, a debt collector. Or most likely a drug dealer not got his money.

As harsh as it was, these types of women mixed with all sorts of dubious characters and subsequently as sad and unnecessary that it was, sometimes this was the consequences of their own deviant behaviour.

Not that anyone deserved to die, the fact of the matter was that they sometimes did and he and his team were left to pick up the pieces.

Tomorrow was another day he thought hopefully they would have something from the pathologist then and be able to move forward a little, even catch him, clear another degenerate citizen off the streets of Leicester.

He would have liked to have seen Tanya tonight, but Fridays and Sunday's were their 'buddy nights" they'd agreed on that from the beginning of their relationship.

Only one problem with that, he had no buddies, so was left to spend these nights on his own. He didn't have the time or inclination for male bonding, and in his eyes females were for laying not for camaraderie.

He liked Tanya, he wouldn't say that he was in love with her, he'd never been in love with anyone in his life, wasn't quite sure what love was, but he enjoyed her company, she made him laugh and in his job there was very little to laugh about.

For a therapist though she didn't discuss much about her own life or her childhood, he had managed to get out of her once that she was an only child and that her parents had died when she was three in a car crash. She had been raised by her Grandparents who had died when she was twenty one, leaving her an orphan with no family.

She had changed the subject very quickly. She was a good at that he thought, going off on a tangent when she wanted to avoid a topic of conversation that she wasn't comfortable with.

She would answer a question with a question too if she wanted to sidestep an uncomfortable query, he'd told her that she should have been a lawyer.

She was a mysterious woman alright, probably the reason he was attracted to her, he hated the predictable, women who told you their life story on their first date, moaned about their ex husbands and nagged like washer women by the third date.

Tanya was not like that; she had never mentioned any ex partners and never nagged.

He'd asked her once about children and she had made it quite clear that kids were not part of her life plan, she had no interest in having them. Full stop and changed the subject as quick as most of his other girlfriends had dropped their knickers. He'd never raised it again because it wasn't part of his life plan either.

Nor was marriage, he'd made that decision early in his career, he was married to his job and he'd learned very early on that being in the police force and marriage did not mix. He'd seen too many of his colleagues divorce because of the demands of the job, left with just a cardboard box of meagre belongings after years of marriage and alimony payments for kids they no longer saw which crippled them.

Women could be so selfish; have no understanding of the demands of the job, there were three divorces on his team when that young girl's body was found near Leicester Forest East about twenty years ago. His men had to work all hours, manning the phone lines, doing door to door enquiries and collecting DNA samples from all the local men between a certain age. This had been the first time DNA was used in an investigation and so they were being closely scrutinised by the media, the top dogs, and politicians alike.

You'd think with it being a young girl murdered that they'd have little bit of empathy, give a little bit of leeway but no all they were concerned about was having their husbands at their beck and call.

No, marriage was definitely not on the cards for him. It was far too much agro. As long as he had a regular shag buddy he was happy.

He would never have considered using prostitutes, he never had it was too risky. He couldn't risk having someone he had slept with being arrested he'd never live it down with the guys at work, he'd lose their respect, and that's one thing he had, their respect. They may not like him, might not like some of the decisions he made, but he had their respect and that was important to him.

Was that what she was, Tanya, a shag buddy? He thought earnestly, she was more than that he reconsidered. He liked her lot, knew very little about her, but time would change that he believed.

They never talked about anything other than at a superficial level at the moment, nothing deep and meaningful. They just enjoyed each other's company and the sex of course. It wasn't earth shattering for him or her he would guess. It was cosy and a release of pent up stress, which was good enough for him, he didn't really want nights of acrobatics; he didn't really want to put that much effort in.

They never talked about each other's work, past, present come to think of it what did they talk about?

He shrugged, what the hell she was a nice, genuine girl, his gut told him that and he could always rely on his gut.

He pulled up outside his cottage, locked the car and looked forward to relaxing in front of the television with a nice drink or two, or three.

Put the week behind him. It had been a long week.

Stephens's cottage was cosy; he'd brought it ten years ago when house prices were low. At the same time he had also brought antique furniture to go with the style and year it was built. He still had that same furniture; he was never at home enough for there to be much wear and tear. He'd not overdone it though, it wasn't cluttered. He hated clutter and hated just as much needless ornaments.

It was detached, and in a cul de sac of five other cottages with enough space between each cottage to not stifle one another. He didn't mix with neighbours much and wanted to be far enough away from his neighbours not to have to. This suited him just fine.

He popped on his CD player and the disc already in place began mellowing out the soft tones of 'Catherine Jenkins' he loved classical music; they were the bulk of his collection.

To the dulcet tones of his favourite singer, he began preparing a microwave dinner all he could be bothered to muster up, trying to chew over the last few days events.

They must have missed something he thought, there can't be zero information. There was always something, something they could get their teeth into, he had a good team, they would follow up every lead, but the limited leads they had, had lead to nothing. He was left feeling ineffectual, nothing constructive to send his team out to investigate on Monday and his Chief wasn't going to be very pleased about that.

He thought back to the note left with the body, maybe there was something more to that, some sort of clue "Guess who" was that a message for them or for her, or for someone close to her, a boyfriend perhaps, that no-one knew about.

The ex husband was coming back early and should land in England tomorrow and he was coming in to be interviewed perhaps something might come out of that, some further leads.

He finished his meal and fell asleep in the warmth of his living room, lulled by the soft voice of Catherine Jenkins.

Chapter Six

My memories haunt me day and night now; the dreams are no longer pleasant ones. I have no respite at all from the horrors that she put me through.

I am two or three years old, still in my pram, so maybe younger. We were going to the park, I was excited I didn't even know what the park was but I was still excited. She wasn't very happy, my clothes were creased I had to look my best she'd said.

"What sort of mother am I to take my son to the park in creased clothes?"

She had taken the iron out of the cupboard and plugged it in. I sat quietly, even at this age I knew that I had to be quiet, listening to the hissing of the water in the iron as it was heating up, watching her putting together a picnic of ham and cheese and blackcurrant juice.

I watched as she preened herself, admiring herself in the cracked mirror standing on the window ledge. I smelt the lemon perfume as she over indulged and the fumes drifted into my pram, and me trying to stifle a cough so as not to annoy her.

Then it happened.

She sprayed the steam onto my white cotton shirt, the creases dropping out as the heat of the vapour touched the fine material, the smile on her face as her little boy was beginning to look well turned-out.

Then I screamed, I screamed louder than I have ever screamed before as the mist of burning heat touched my skin.

Gut Instinct

She had ironed my shirt with me still in it!

The pain was agonising, the physical and psychological scars are still a constant reminder of the one and only day that we went to the park.

Oh, yes we still went, there was a man who went there every Saturday you see, took his own child. He was a divorcee and these were his access visits. Mother thought she had a chance with him, but I spoilt it for her – I couldn't stop crying, no matter how hard I tried the pain was just too much.

The man, he left the park soon after we arrived, couldn't stand my crying, I drove him away, as no man was going to want my mother with a screaming baby in tow, were they?

At least that was what she said.

For days after she would scream at me, torture me; refuse to feed me because of what I had done.

I didn't care I was drifting in and out of sleep, shivers one minute and overwhelming heat the next.

This I think was when I had my first of many dreams, pleasant dreams, dreams of snow and dreams of rain pouring down on to my body, feeling the coldness on my face and on the wound that still remains today.

****

I'd watched her for awhile that night, gyrating her body on the dance floor, enjoying the perverted attention of the men in the room, throwing her head back in laughter, enjoying herself while her child was most probably left alone at home, scared and hungry.

I watched most of them on a Friday night in there short skirts suspended above cellulite ridden legs, their low tops abundant with saggy stretch marked breasts, and their grotesque over made up faces, trying to hide their wrinkled, aged features.

They were just like her, just like her.

I watched them pick up men, I followed them to their neglected homes and saw them seduce and have sex with this wanton species.

She'd let me in as soon as she had seen the tears, made me a cup of tea. Tea and sympathy that's what I got. Tea and fucking sympathy! If only she'd given me that all those years ago, instead of sour milk and maltreatment.

Did she think I was going to let her off, forgive her now she was being nice. It was too late bitch. It was far too late.

Her house was a mess, dinner pots still left on the draining board, the stale remnants of food becoming hard on the plates.

Where was the child, there was no cupboard under the stairs, nowhere to hide him, but he'd be there he knew it, she'd perhaps found a new hiding place by now.

Afterwards, I gave her the card.

"There you go mother, a mother's day card, I made it for you, see I didn't forget this year. I remembered."

I remembered every year after my tenth birthday; the scars would not let me forget. I kept a notebook and marked off 365 days, no way was I going to be tortured again for missing something I didn't even know existed until then.

I hadn't known what I was in trouble for at the time, but I had known I was in trouble, she made me eat my food off the floor, said I was no better than a stray dog on the streets.

While I was doing this distasteful act, lapping my food up as quickly as I could, she stuck a poker up my backside.

"That's what giving birth is like son and if you can't fucking reward me for what I went through for you, then you're scum, do you hear me scum!"

This was because I hadn't made her a mother's day card, hadn't acknowledged all she did for me.

So 365 days later I made her one, copied one out of a magazine, cello taped flowers onto a piece of card and wrote inside, presented it to her with pride.

Only I was in trouble again, it was Monday, mother's day was yesterday, I'd forgotten again................

Chapter Seven

Monday 10th March

Monday morning Stephen had arrived bright and early and he had given his instructions to his team as they arrived in. Paul was a little downcast, but he would get over it. He needed to toughen up if he was to survive the police force.

Derek and John were joking around as usual, this was how they survived, they were able to add humour into their day, and you couldn't stay serious all the time with the things that they had to deal with on a daily basis.

Humour kept you sane.

"Any girl can be glamorous" Derek was saying to Vera, the only girl on Stephen's team.

"All you have to do is stand still and look stupid"

At that point Vera's pen went flying through the air, hitting Paul on the nose.

"What the fuck......" he yelled, as Vera, Derek and John stood frozen but desperately trying to stifle their giggles.

"Well that's the fun over for now"

Stephen walked in knowing that someone had to defuse this situation, and that someone needed to be him. Paul was not in a great mood as it was and had looked ready to boil over at any time.

"Paul," he added "What time did Jane's ex say he would be arriving"

"About lunchtime sir, if there were no flight delays, he's due to land at East Midlands about eleven fifteen"

"Okay, you and Vera can interview him when he comes in, but take it gentle he's not a suspect and his son has just lost his mother, I'm sure there is some paperwork you can be getting on with in the meantime"

"Sir" they both said in unison, and then headed for their desks to do just that.

"Derek, John"

"Sir"

"Go see the sister again, see if she can think of anything else of significance now she's calmed down a little........ Oh, and if she asks about the funeral tell her we will let her know as soon as the coroner can release the body. We'll all meet back here at four thirty for a debrief."

"Sir" they both replied looking completely downhearted.

He knew he was possibly sending them on a wild goose chase, they knew that too, but what more could they do, but follow their tail's until something fresh came along, some new evidence they could follow.

It was a waste sending such proficient members of his team on house calls, but what else could he do, for now.

The rest of the team he sent to speak with some of the onlookers that had spoken with the uniform guys just to clarify what they had said and to see if they had anything more to add, it was amazing how many people remembered something the day after but couldn't be bothered to ring the police.

Maybe he should have sent Derek and John to do that and the others to speak with the neighbours he thought, but it was too late now they were out the door.

He liked Derek and John, they had been on his team since he started, he had head hunted them from another section, and they'd always worked well for him, respected him. He had a lot of time for them both; they were two of his best detectives.

They had both worked together as a team now for four years and they were good, they were extremely good and obtained good results.

They were a double act, and double acts were how two officers worked together in the police. The good cop, bad cop routines were often a standing joke but it was true and it worked.

Derek had a shaved head and lived and died in jeans, he was the tough looking cop. The one the cons were wary of. Whereas, John he was the smooth looking cop, looked more like he should be working at the stock exchange than the police force in his designer suits. He looked the softer of the two, the one the cons would warm too and look desperately at for support, the one that they always felt safe with.

But nothing could be further than the truth; Derek was the softie and John the tough one.

Derek was physically tough, but John was psychologically tough.

This confused villains, they'd have their eye on Derek, waiting for him to pounce, and then when they least expected it John would pounce, throwing them completely off balance, and this is when the truth would often come out. The con would be completely confused and disorientated; this was when they would say something they were desperately trying not to say.

Derek was forty eight years old, married with three children. He had just remarried and his new wife had a good work ethic.

She was a buyer for an international department store. She supported Derek's commitment to his job and understood this as she was just as committed to her career as he was his. This had been lacking in his previous marriages.

Stephen had gone to their wedding and they were a couple well and truly besotted to one another. She was a good looking girl, with a figure most girls would die for. Quite a catch, Stephen had thought and was unsure how Derek had managed to catch her, but hey ho at least he was settled now and could put all his energies into his job.

Derek had spent most of his career in the police force working towards joining the plain clothes division and before joining Stephen's team had been doing undercover work for the vice squad.

John was married too, to his childhood sweetheart. They had had just celebrated their twenty fifth wedding anniversary, which is unusual for coppers.

John's wife was a stay at home mum to their two children and supportive of his profession. She was a pretty girl, intelligent and self sufficient. She kept the home fires burning while John concentrated on his career. Stephen had no doubt that John would be sitting in his seat in a few years time if he himself got the promotion that he was hoping for.

John had previously worked in the money laundering and counterfeit money division. He was a hard worker and had taken more than a few felons' off the streets.

Stephen was lucky to have them on his team.

Chapter Eight

It was ten past four when the telephone rang on Stephen's desk. It was Owen Jameson, the pathologist.

"Hi Owen, what you got for me?" he asked praying that he had something.

"Definitely suffocation from the pillow Stephen and my thoughts about time of death are spot on. No DNA though I'm afraid, nothing on her, looks like this guy kept his distance, nothing in her nails so doesn't look like she put up any fight."

71

"No sexual assault?" Stephen asked feeling more and more depressed as the day went on.

"No sexual assault" he replied.

"So what the hell did he kill her for" he said more to himself than to Owen.

"That's your job Stephen, not mine" he responded amusingly "But I do have something for you"

"What?" asked Stephen sitting up straight in his chair, all ears.

"We've had the toxicology reports in; there was alcohol in her system......."

"That figures" Stephen said cutting him off mid flow and beginning to sink down in his chair again. "She had been on a night out"

"................And Rohypnol"

Stephen checked he had heard right and had put the phone down after thanking Owen for his help and asking him to inform the family if and when the body could be released for burial.

Rohypnol he pondered the date rape drug with no rape, but was there a date?

She clearly knew her attacker, there had been no forced entry and she had not put up any form of resistance. Well now we know possibly why?

Stephen looked up, his team were gathered in the office and were all looking at him. He looked at his watch four forty five, he was late.

He had got so wrapped up in his thoughts, he'd lost track of time. He jumped up and made his way to the main office, carrying some interesting news and wondering if they had anything new for him.

****

Stephen was driving home on auto pilot, deep in thought. He'd not left the office until six forty five. His staff meeting had run on longer than he had expected.

Paul and Vera had interviewed Jane's ex and he had a cast iron alibi, being in Germany at the time of the murder, not that he was a prime suspect but it's always best to check these things out. Often the first port of call in these cases was the husband or estranged husband as he was.

He had told them that he had no idea who could have done this, did not know of any enemies that Jane might have and was unquestionably distraught by what had happened.

The positive was that he was now going to quit his job and bring up his little boy, that was his first priority now, and he was keen to be kept informed on how the investigation was going.

Or not going. Stephen thought still exasperated by how little evidence they had.

Derek and John had revisited the sister and she had been pleased to see them, she was going to call them as something had crossed her mind.

About four weeks ago Jane had been involved in an affray in her son's school playground with another mother.

Jane had been quite upset at the time because this was not her style, to be fighting in a school playground. A classmate of her sons had been bullying him and Jane was quite sensitive about bullying as she had been bullied at school herself.

She'd approached the boy's mother and attempted to speak with her to try and amicably sort things out. The other mother had turned vicious though and began pushing and shoving Jane, to which Jane responded by fighting her back.

The other mother who had the reputation of being a bit of a 'hard nut' had come off the worse, and Jane's sister wondered if the humiliation had caused her to go round and kill her sister.

It was a long shot but Derek and John had gone round to see this mother, whose words had been

"Karma," when they informed her of who they were and why they had called.

However this woman had been at an engagement party on the night in question and had provided Derek and John with the details of other people that could clarify this, one of those being a lawyer who was a cousin to the potential groom.

He had remembered her well; he made quite disparaging remarks about her behaviour on the night, "made a right show of herself" he had said.

The party had gone on until the early hours and she had been flat out on the floor highly intoxicated when the lawyer had left at around 4 a.m. So the lads didn't think this was anything they needed to follow up any further.

The rest of his team had chased up other witnesses and nothing of great value there.

This case was becoming like a nightmare; the priority of the homicide division was to get murderers off the street and usually with all cases there was something, some small titbit that when investigated lead to something else and eventually they had an arrest, but this one was not providing even a morsel of information to follow up.

Stephen had updated them on the pathologists report and they had revisited the case once again.

No-one could quite 'get' why someone had given her a date rape drug and yet not raped her.

"Perhaps it was to subdue her" Vera had contributed "Stop her from struggling while he killed her"

"He went along to kill her, it was definitely pre-mediated, to be carrying Rohypnol" Paul added "and of course the .... erm card he left"

"Maybe then this guy didn't have the certainty that he would be able to overpower her" John added.

"She was seven stone nothing John most guys would be able to overpower her" Derek questioned.

"Maybe it wasn't a guy" said Paul.

The room went silent for a moment, while people contemplated this fact.

Vera broke the silence, "Girls don't usually carry around a date rape drug, maybe it was just a small guy, there's plenty of you around" she said teasingly looking directly at Derek.

This went on for nearly two hours and Stephen had left feeling that they were no further forward than they had been at the beginning.

They were just going around in circles, so he had called it a night and sent them home.

What the hell was going on here he thought are people closing ranks?   Are the public frightened to say anything for fear of repercussions?

There was something going on he knew that but just couldn't quite put his finger on it.

Somebody somewhere must know something and if anyone was going to get to the bottom of it he was.

He pulled up at his destination and turned off the ignition and at the same time turned off his mind, something he had learned to do, otherwise this job would send you insane.

<u>Chapter Nine</u>

Vera was feeling really perturbed when she arrived home after her shift. Being the only girl on the team she saw herself as the sensitive one, the mother figure even though she was not old enough to be any of their mothers.

She was forty years of age but didn't look it. She had inherited youthful genes, or so she thought because she never really used face creams or paid any particular attention to her skin.

She had blonde curly hair that drove her mad at times but would be what most girls would give their high teeth for. Brown eyes, a petite figure and Kate Winslet style lips that most men wanted to kiss.

She hadn't got much time for men, much to their disappointment, she'd had one very bad relationship and that had put her off for life and so therefore had dedicated her life and her love to her job, becoming a little bit of a feminist too.

She was not enjoying her work so much these days though, they were a good team but since Paul had joined the team things had become a little tense.

It wasn't Paul; although he could be a pain in the arse sometimes when he had his intellectual head on, it was Stephen.

He had taken such a dislike to Paul and showed his feelings whenever he had the chance, unnecessarily humiliating him in meetings.

It didn't help that Derek and John took the Mickey out of him too, behind his back, they had worked their way up the ladder and didn't take to kindly to this 'bookworm' joining the team.

If only they knew what she knew about Paul, he wasn't always an intellectual, in fact far from it.

Vera didn't rate this type of behaviour; she believed that they all had to work together so therefore should treat each other with respect.

We were all different and she believed that this enabled everyone to bring something unique to the table.

Vera had experienced a difficult childhood, things she kept to herself, things that she tried not to think about or it would drive her mad. However this made her ultra sensitive to other people's feelings.

In her training the senior officer had told her that she had 'too much empathy' and needed to lose that if she was going to make it as a copper.

Vera hadn't taken this on board as she had disagreed with it and believed that her understanding of people's feelings made her a good copper and thought that too many in the force had very little compassion.

Certainly her experience of the police in her younger days hadn't been a pleasant one; they had shown no compassion for her.

Vera wanted to be different and she wanted to make a difference, so the unhelpful criticism she had received in training was dumped right where it belonged, in the bin.

She'd thought about addressing her boss about his behaviour towards Paul and telling him how uncomfortable this was for the rest of the team and how uncompassionate he was being.

Normally Vera would have no qualms about doing this, she was not one to hold things in and let them fester, but she didn't want to give him any excuse to go against her.

She needed to stay on this case and keep on top of the information that was coming in and she knew Stephen well, if you challenged him, and he didn't like it then for a while he would let you know that he wasn't happy, would put you on menial jobs and withhold information that she needed to hear right now.

Paul had hit the nail on the head, when he said that it was a serial killer, she agreed with him entirely but was not going to be seen to be agreeing with him, and she wanted to be an important member of the team when the next bodies turned up, which they would she knew that.

Stephen Roberts was not the only one with a good intuition; she had a well practised gut instinct too.

She'd had to develop one to survive her childhood.

Her stomach churned when she thought of those times, it was surprising she had done well at all, but look at her now, she had her own home, a good job and she was happy.

Vera was the computer whizz, and that was the gift she brought to the team, anything that needed research, or if computers needed hacking she was 'man for the job'.

Problem was she had a morbid curiosity; in fact she was downright nosey and in her spare time liked to research her colleagues.

She would look into their private lives because she perceived that she needed to be one step ahead of them all the time.

Vera felt that knowledge was important, the more knowledge you had about people and things, the more powerful you were.

She had accrued a lot of information about her colleagues, knew a lot of things about them, things from their past and present and regularly kept an eye on their computer activities.

'Oh yes' she thought 'if ever they managed to get anything on me, then I would have enough on them to persuade them to keep their mouths shut'.

Vera did not want her past coming out, she didn't want peoples sympathy, she didn't want to lose her tough girl image and boy didn't you need to be tough to survive working with seven men. You needed thick skin, very thick skin indeed.

Her tough image all the same was a show, she knew this, she knew that it was her protection from being hurt, it was her survival mechanism that she had developed at a very young age, and one she would find difficult to let go of, and besides it didn't harm anyone, most people liked her and it kept her safe.

Her mind wandered back to Jane Smith, poor girl to die so young. But at least it had not been a violent death; at least she had not suffered. Her children will be looked after by their Dad, they will be alright, and he seemed a good sort.

And the card, the card said.

"GUESS WHO"

Guess who indeed she thought.

Chapter Ten

Friday 21st March

It had been a long day for Lizzie, the kids had driven her to despair and she was absolutely desperate for a 'shag'. It had been over a month since she'd last had one and she felt like her private parts were like a dam waiting to burst. A month was quite a long time for her.

Most of the time they were one night stands but at least she got laid. She would have liked a steady relationship but it didn't seem to happen. She could never seem to meet anyone that wanted a long term relationship but plenty that wanted sex.

She was running her 'so called best friend' Carol's words through her head, trying to ignore the incessant fighting of her three little ones in the perpetually untidy living room whilst cooking chicken nuggets for their tea .

Carol had told her to make them wait, that she would never find somebody permanent if she slept with them on the first night. "Men will sleep with girls like you" she'd said "but don't want to marry them". Lizzie had felt quite annoyed at first, insulted in fact. It was okay for her to talk, she was married to a handsome guy with plenty of money, she had it on bloody tap, but she knew deep down that Carol was right. She was always right, self righteous bitch that she was.

"Shut the fuck up" she screamed as the noise grew louder and louder in the living room, "bloody kids."

Lizzie had three kids all under six years old, all by different partners and they were the results of one night stands.

The fathers hadn't wanted to know when she'd tracked them down and told them that she was pregnant. One even accused her of it not being his, as if? But she'd managed fine without the arse holes up to now and it was their loss. As much as they did her head in sometimes, they were great kids and she loved them to bits.

Lizzie and Carol had been best friends since school. Carol was always the pretty one, the more sensible one and the one that all the lads wanted. They'd hover around her like bees on honey, and only if Carole turned them down would they then turn their attention to Lizzie. It had been a bug bear to Lizzie and even more depressing that her best friend's life had turned out so fabulous and hers so challenging, so empty and so bloody lonely. Here she was stuck with three kids and no man and not a penny from any of their fathers.

It never ceased to amaze her or her friends on how she had managed to get up the duff by three bloody Houdini's. Disappearing off the face of the earth to avoid the CSA and not wanting any responsibility for their children.

The screams from the living room went through her, she felt as if her nerves were shattered this week, she just wanted to fill their faces with food, get them off to her mothers, so that she could get some peace and get ready for her one night out a week.

She went out every Friday night with the girls to this club in town, Jason's. It was supposedly for the "over thirties, but some of the women that frequented the place were not a day younger than fifty.

"I don't want to be still doing that scene at fifty" she thought "still looking for a man, when you're old and saggy, that's sad."

This made her desperate, she was beginning to think that life was passing her by, she was thirty eight and still there was no long term relationship, she was beginning to notice the lines around her eyes and on her forehead getting deeper, and last week had spotted the beginnings of cellulite on her backside.

Once these got worse, who would want to sleep with her then she thought, not even aware that people still would – older men would, they aged too. If this had crossed her mind she would have been mortified at the thought. In her eyes her love life was closer to the end than the beginning and if she didn't find someone soon she would be left on the shelf a rotting old spinster.

She was looking forward to tonight though she'd followed her friend's unwanted and certainly unasked for advice and deprived herself of the only bloody comfort she ever got in her life, apart from her fags and drink that is, and had abstained for a month now. But if she had it her way tonight was the night she thought a smile spreading across her face.

For the past three weeks she'd been having a bit of a dance with this bloke called Ivan, well to be honest a little bit more than that, a bit of a snog and a bit of a feel too, although she wouldn't admit that to Carol. If her luck was in tonight would be the night, she'd already decided that, just as she had naively decided that this one could be it, the one that swept her off her feet, took on her and the kids and loved them just as much as she did.

She'd waited long enough for a shag, surely he'd want more than that now, and besides she was gagging for it, and she knew he was too. If she didn't give it him tonight, he'd probably be off flirting with someone else, someone a little less frigid.

"Tea's up you three" she shouted and held her breath in anticipation of the usual squabbles about who was sitting where and who had more than the other.

****

The kids were now dropped off at her mothers with the usual excitement, noise and her mother's weekly repeated ranting about picking them up before midday, she was not gonna be babysitting all day while she was in bed recovering from an hangover, she'd droned, oh and that she had a life too.

What life, she never left the flipping house since Dad died! Never-the-less Lizzie did her usual "Yes mam, no problem mam" and she left the house as quick as she could get away, to the noise of her her kids fighting over what DVD they were going to watch, and her mam droning on about the time she wanted the kids picking up. God, had she never been young once, she thought fractiously.

Now for a bit of peace and quiet, at least until Brenda came round with the bottle of Lambrini they always drank before they went out.

She ran her bath and noticed that as much as she was looking forward to this night out Lizzie felt anxious, she felt like a cloud was hovering over her. "What the fuck is wrong with me" she thought, counting the days in her head trying to work out her next due date. No she'd got two weeks yet before her periods were due so it was not PMT, surely she wasn't nervous about the inevitable that she'd planned for the end of the night. Maybe it was, it had been a month since she'd last had sex, maybe this was what it was like, feeling like she was a virgin again.

She laughed out loud as she emerged herself in the steaming hot bubble bath. "I'll be okay once I get some booze down me neck" she thought shaving her nether regions, legs and underarms. My they'd grown.

She'd done this on purpose, not had a shave for a few weeks and had worn the knickers she'd had on for two days when she'd gone out.

It was a deterrent for her, she thought twice about having sex when she knew she smelt and had pubic hairs she could plait. She knew that even if she was as hot as a monkey on heat, she would not do it unless she was clean and shaved. This was her willpower and it had worked a treat. Ivan would think she was a 'nice girl' now.

Peace at last she pondered. She loved her kids to bits, but god were they noisy; she looked forward to her Friday nights and getting a bit of noiseless peace before her heavy night out. It was utter bliss.

She'd spoke too soon she thought as she heard the back door open. Bloody Brenda she was early as usual, no peace for the wicked.

"Why do you build me up, build me up buttercup baby then you let me down, let me down" Brenda crooned as she made her way up the stairs.

She couldn't sing for toffee, in fact she couldn't do nowt for toffee Lizzie laughed as she got out of the bath and grabbed her grubby off white dressing gown, from the bathroom door and headed for her bedroom.

"What do ya think" Brenda asked, trying to do her best model girl pose, hips pushed out and hand perched on the door frame of Lizzie's bedroom.

She looked blooming awful as usual. Red Lycra skirt, green top, black fishnet tights and white stiletto boots, she looked like one of Santa's elves, Lizzie thought.

"You look great" she lied.

Brenda never did have much dress sense, she was overweight and never dressed fittingly for her size, but she didn't want to upset her friend not before they went out. She knew that if she told her the truth that she would be on a downer all night – and that would be unbearable. Brenda was the life and soul of any party when she was on an upper, but on a downer she'd ruin the night for everyone.

Lizzie could remember one time her ruining everyone's night by being miserable and agitated, crying over her drink. She wouldn't tell anyone what was up and thrived on the attention of everyone rallying around her trying to cajole her to find out.

At the end of the night when she'd ruined everyone's evening and put them all on a downer too, she'd said

"My goldfish died today" – fucking goldfish died, who cries over a goldfish dying for Pete's sake, they'd all been furious, Lizzie in particularly she only got out once a week and she didn't need it spoiling over a bloody goldfish.

"I'm organising a charity do" Brenda piped in breaking into Lizzie's trip down memory lane.

"Are you?" she asked gobsmacked at Brenda doing anything for anyone but herself.

"Yeh, for people who can't have orgasms" she replied...... letting that sink into Lizzies mind for a moment. Lizzie just looked confused.

"What the......."

"Let me know if you can't come!" she said rolling about laughing, fat wobbling like a beached whale.

Lizzie's eyebrows rose in a questioning,

"what the........". then she clicked on and joined in the laughter.

"What you like" she said "go and open that bottle of wine before I thump ya".

Chapter Eleven

The place was buzzing tonight, and the queue was unusually long to get in. Eventually Brenda and Lizzie paid their admission fee and entered the club, Abba singing Waterloo Road, blared out of the sound system. Lizzie hadn't really liked Abba until she'd watched Mamma Mia, since then the music had grown on her.

They boogied across the dance floor heading to the bar for their usual first drink, a cider and black followed by a whiskey chaser, after the wine that would do just nicely to warm them

100

both up. Lizzie scoured the room for Ivan but couldn't see him yet, it was early still.

"Did you see that guy behind us in the queue Liz" Brenda shouted above the music.

Lizzie shook her head, not wanting to even try to shout over the music. God it was loud tonight.

"He was bloody gorgeous, Liz you shouda' seen him, made my clit twitch".

They both laughed. Brenda was on top form tonight thank god, and she came out with some crackers when she was like this. Please don't win another goldfish at the fair Lizzie thought sniggering to herself.

They both headed for the dance floor, as "Girl I'm gonna make you sweat...." came blasting out.

As the night went on Lizzie thought that Ivan wasn't coming, she had brushed off a few guys tonight that had shown an interest in her and would be well pissed off if he didn't show she thought, because they had all moved on to someone else now, she'd drunk more than usual too, probably down to her nerves she thought.

She was beginning to realise that her expectations in a man were spot on, expect nothing and you won't be disappointed she thought.

"Look at him over there" Brenda piped up, she could see that Lizzie was not her usual happy self

"He's fucking ugly, there's hot sex, fast sex, group sex, leather sex, and telephone sex, but for people with faces like his there's........... Masturbation" she chuckled.

Brenda had been cracking jokes all night and Lizzie was finding it harder and harder to laugh due to her deteriorating mood.

****

The night had been a good one Lizzie thought as she waved Brenda off in a taxi, and now it was gonna get better she shivered as she clung on to Ivan's arm like she feared him escaping.

He hadn't got there until the last hour and she'd begun to think that he wasn't coming. She could feel her mood dropping as the time went on and believed her irrational fears that he had got sick of waiting, and wished that she had given it him sooner. So when he did saunter in without a care in the world and headed straight for her she was elated.

It was fascinating how quickly her mood changed at the sight of him, she'd never let him out of her sight since, even followed him to the toilet. This one was not getting away she thought, not now, not ever.

She didn't even let the lipstick mark on his cheek perturb her for long. Probably some tart trying to kiss him on his way in. she consoled herself with this and was going to stick to it, nothing was going to spoil this night.

They jumped in the next taxi and couldn't keep their hands off each other; she made it clear to him that he was definitely on a promise tonight.

As he was paying the taxi she fumbled nervously with her front door keys. She got more nervous when she liked them a lot, more eager to please, more anxious that her performance would be satisfying enough to keep them hanging about.

He was behind her now, as she entered the house, tearing her clothes from her, gasping and groaning in prolonged anticipation. She dropped her bag on the sofa and fumbled with his flies, feeling for his erection with her groping frantic hands. They fell to the floor naked and he plunged into her like it was his last shag, resembling a mad man believing that she was going to change her mind and push him away when he was at the point of no return.

He bit into her neck overpoweringly at the same time as his whole body convulsed. Then it was all over, within seconds, leaving her feeling frustrated, dissatisfied and fucked off! He climbed off, arrogantly stepping back into his pants and had the audacity to ask her if she'd got anything to eat. No apology, there was no humiliation or awkwardness or any embarrassment at his premature ejaculation.

"That was good" he said emerging himself into her sofa with no apparent comprehension of what he had just done.

She dawdled in the kitchen, trying to calm down, four fucking weeks without a shag and then when I get one it wasn't worth the effort she thought. She made him a potted beef sandwich contemplating whether to spit in it and then made excuses that she was tired, and that he needed to go, and "yes, of course she would meet up with him next week, she was looking forward to it."

She went to bed feeling depressed and lonely yet again, minus one orgasm!

She tossed and turned in bed, both with sexual frustration and her mind doing somersaults.

What now she thought, she'd put all her money on him, had high hopes, she'd gone off him big time now. It wasn't just the sex, they could have perhaps worked on that, it was his bloody arrogance. That'll teach her to put all her eggs in one basket!

Twenty minutes later, the door went. What's he want now she thought as she got up to answer it. I kept my mouth shut earlier, but I won't now, I'll give the arrogant bastard what for!

Chapter Twelve

"Another one bites the dust" he thought rubbing his hands together in excitement. I enjoyed this one, she'd been easy to dupe, big tits and colossal empathy this one had. Fell for my sob story like a good 'un. It had been quick too, quicker than the last one, probably down to all the drink she'd had.

I've been watching her for months, just like all the others and she was one of the biggest tarts I have seen down Jason's, different man every week, rubbing herself indiscreetly up and down their bodies well before the last dance. What was the matter with these girls had they no pride. A real fucking tease she was, knew she'd have them by the short and curlies and in her bed by the end of the night. Men were weak always had been when it came to their cocks, didn't care where they dipped them as long as they dipped them.

And more than a hundred had dipped them in my mother!

My mind never lets me forget my childhood and my mother, although lord knows how she could be called anyone's mother. Biggest tart of the lot, I wish someone had snuffed her lights out and I'd been adopted by some 'Mary Poppins' style mother how different my life would have been. Maybe then I would have been happy with who I was.

I absentmindedly rub the scar on my forehead remembering that day as vividly as if it was yesterday.

I'd been about seven years old and she'd had her usual Friday night out at the local working men's club and had left me on my own again, something she had been doing since I was five.

Gut Instinct

She'd brought home yet another Friday night guy, obviously just wanting one thing as per usual. She could never remember their names, but this one I could, his name I will never forget.

This man scarred me for life, the memories send a shiver down my spine. I doubt he'd know the damage he caused not now, doubt he'd even care.

She had come into my bedroom and as I stirred had said "Don't fucking leave this bedroom in the morning pig face, not until I call you. I like this one and I want him to get to know me and like me back before he meets you and runs a fucking mile, do ya hear"

I nodded, still half asleep. This was what I had learned to do, nod at anything she said. It was always a request of me, never an offer so most the time I knew that I had to say 'yes' it became my natural response to everything she said rather than get battered or worse.

The usual grunting, panting and screaming noises had come rumbling through the thin walls and I'd known that I wouldn't get any sleep till it was all over. Sometimes it would go on all night, but that night it hadn't.

Part of me had wished it had, and then I wouldn't have fallen into such a deep sleep.

The next morning I'd woken up soaked through, I had wet the bed again, my heart sank, and I knew now for sure that I was going to get a battering, this petrified me.

I looked at my Mickey Mouse clock on my bedside table and it was only eight o'clock, if she was still asleep I could get the sheets in the washer/dryer and then when she crawled back to bed after her lover had left, which she usually did, I could put them back on the bed again.

I'd crept downstairs, no smells of bacon drifted up which was a good sign, I knew her usual pattern by then, you see. She would give them the fuck of their life, then cook them a breakfast to show off her homemaking skills. Sure that this would make them want her. There were no sounds of false laughter, the house was silent, another good sign.

Gut Instinct

I'd walked into the kitchen bottomless, only wearing my pyjama top which was two inches too short for me, the smelly, stained sheets dragging behind me.

I'd switched on the light and stood there petrified, there she was in her dressing gown sat on his knee kissing him, for seconds they didn't notice me, too engrossed in their immoral act and I thought I might just be able to turn around and go back upstairs. But it was too late they had both looked up and had seen me. Her face instantaneously screwed up in rage and he, the man, had just rolled about laughing at the sight before his eyes. Pointing at something a stranger should never have seen.

She'd told me not to go downstairs but I hadn't known she'd be up yet. I could tell she was furious and he, the man, had found my half nakedness funny, he'd laughed at me, howled in fact pointing as if I had three balls,

I ran back upstairs in shame, mortified that my boyhood had been laughed at and that I'd wet the bed at the perceived grown up age of seven, and this guy had thought it funny.

I didn't know which had been worse, the shame or the battering that I got ten minutes later after the guy had abruptly left, telling her she perhaps needed to sort her son out, she hadn't even been able to give him one of her special breakfasts.

Once again it had been my entire fault; the guy would never come back now after I had humiliated her.

She hit me so hard that she'd split my head open, would have needed ten stitches at least if she'd been good enough to take me to the hospital, but no just gave me a bandage and told me to wrap it around my head and shut up whining.

This was when I first began to hate my penis, began to think that it <u>wasn't</u> normal, that there <u>was</u> something wrong with it, something wrong with me.

I had known I was different, known I wasn't happy with myself, known that the dangly bit between my legs shouldn't be there. I'd known that for the last few years, I wasn't a stupid child, but this was the beginning of my compulsive urge to cut it off.

Gut Instinct

This was also when my mother started to lock me in the 'bobby hole', the cupboard under the stairs, on a Friday night, sometimes for nineteen hours at a time, depending how long her visitors stayed.

I hated that bobby hole, it was dark, damp and full of spiders, huge spiders that might eat me alive, there were monsters in there too, I felt them brush against my legs in the dark, had seen the shadows on the wall. I had to keep still, quiet, so the monsters wouldn't know I was there.

I heard a man once ask my mother where her child was as they were going up the stairs; she'd said that I was staying at my dad's for the weekend. This had confused me, she'd always told me that I had never had a Dad, that I was born without a Dad. That God had said I wasn't good enough to have a Dad. Because of my deformity she'd said. That must have been that thing between my legs.

I was glad anyway that he hadn't sent me a Dad if they were anything like that man that had laughed at me, but who was having the last laugh now eh.

My mother used to say

"He, who laughs last, laughs longest"

I'm having the longest laugh now.

That was it that would be what I could put on one of her cards, but not the next one, I have got just the card that I   want to leave next time, the card that would let him know that it was 'me!'.

Chapter Thirteen

Saturday 22nd 3.15p.m.

Stephen was dozing on the settee, an old movie still blaring away on the T.V. when he awoke to a shrill sound. It took him awhile to come too and to register the noise, just when he came to the realisation of what it was, the phone stopped.

He plodded into the kitchen and put the coffee machine on, his mouth as dry as a camels arse when the phone rang again.

"Ho" he grunted annoyed at having been woken up from quite an erotic dream.

"It's me serg" a voice he vaguely recognised "you'd better get down here straight away.

"Why?" he asked still not quite adjusted to being awake.

"There's been another one."

It was Derek he suddenly realised he sounded out of breath.

"Another What Derek?" he asked "since when have I chrysalised into mystic meg?"

"Another girl sir, another murder"

Stephen tried to stay calm, two murders in the space of two weeks that can't be right, it must be a co-incidence. They hadn't even solved the last one yet, they had come to a dead end.

"Tell me the details Derek" he asked putting on his shoes and trying to remember where he'd left his car keys.

"She was suffocated again sir with a pillow. This one has a bite mark on her neck though boss, so we may well have some DNA to go on.

"Oh well that's something" he sighed with relief, he couldn't go to his boss with a 'no result' on this one too.

"There's something else boss" Derek said, alerting Stephen away from his liberating thoughts.

"What?!" he asked. He was getting a little pissed off with having to pull teeth out of Derek for information.

"He's left another card"

****

Stephen put the phone down after getting the crime scene details and telling Derek that he was on his way. He was in shock.

That nonce had been right all along, it was a serial killer.

117

Could there really be a serial killer in a mediocre city like Leicester. This was beginning to feel a little out of his depth.

This was the stuff you read about in books or saw on television, it didn't happen in real life surely.

He'd have to ring Tanya cancel tonight, this was going to be a long night he could sense it, and he'd ring and order her some flowers,

It was essential that he get the pathologist to rush this autopsy through they needed to catch this man before he killed again, and then there was the card, his thoughts were soaring from one thing to another. What was that supposed to mean?

"Another one bites the dust"

That was no clue, just some psycho gloating that he'd done it again.

"Stop panicking!" he said out loud to himself, as he reversed his car out of his driveway, it is probably just a copycat. There had been enough information in the Mercury for someone to imitate the other murder.

He whizzed through the traffic, as irritable drivers honked their horn at him, unaware of his haste or that he was a police officer.

He was heading for the Hepburn estate, a relatively new council estate, built around a small shopping precinct and leisure centre that prided itself on a pool with a wave machine and twenty five foot enclosed water slide.

The estate had its own police station and undoubtedly some of the staff from there would be on the scene, in all probability were the first response, but this was too big for them, it would be left to his department to pick up this one.

'The card' he recalled, sitting upright in his seat, 'the calling card' as Paul had called it. That was not in the Mercury, no-one but his team knew about the 'calling card.'

119

It incensed him that Paul could be right and he continued to try and find evidence in his mind that this was a copycat.

He pulled up as close as he could to the familiar black and yellow tape and walked to the relatively modest council house, not so many onlookers this time, he thought.

He flashed his warrant card to the officer standing outside; just as an overwhelming feeling of déjà vu hit his stomach.

The usual buzz was going on as was expected at a murder scene, however this time he could hear kids voices, coming from the kitchen.

He walked in and sitting at the well used looking pine breakfast table were a middle aged woman, a female police officer that he didn't know, a woman in her mid thirties still in her pyjamas, and much to his disgust running around the kitchen, making as much noise as they possibly could were four young and very boisterous children.

"Whose are these children" he asked compellingly.

"One's mine" said the thirty something woman

"The other three are the erm girls" the police officer said nodding her head towards the living room, not wanting to say deceased.

"And you are?" he asked the middle aged woman, noticing the distress in her face and wishing he'd been a little gentler.

"This is the mother sir" responded the police woman "She is the one that called us sir"

Stephen got the message, she must have found the body he liked this officer immediately, she was well trained, not like some of them didn't know their arses from their heads.

"Okay" Stephen said, hoping to get this place into some kind of order.

"Miss?" he asked looking at the younger girl.

"I'm Lucy, I live next door" she replied.

"Okay Lucy, could you do me a big, big favour, would you take your child and the erm..... the other three round to your home, whilst we talk to................" He looked at the other woman, her face distorted in grief.

"This is Mrs Wright" the officer offered pleasantly.

"Okay, while I talk to Mrs Wright"

Lucy agreed although Stephen could see it was reluctantly, she'd wanted to be part of the action naturally, this was normal human behaviour she didn't want to miss anything.

"We'll come round and have a chat with you in a while" he added, seeing her face cheer up immediately.

"Come on kids" she shouted as she scrambled them all together and left through the back door.

Peace at last he thought; now I know why I don't want kids.

He went into the living room and for the second time in two weeks he saw a dead girl lying on her living room floor with Owen checking the body and men and women in white overalls checking the scene.

For Stephen it felt unreal.

Chapter Fourteen

Stephen was on his way back to the station, it would be another weekend that his officers had to give up their leave, that wouldn't be very healthy for the perpetrator, when, and he knew it would be WHEN he was caught, his officers would not be gentle with him, that he also knew for certain.

What had they got?

Lizzie had been to Jason's, was that a coincidence or was there something to that.

Her mother had been babysitting Lizzie's three children at her home; they had been dropped off the evening before. She had appeared happy and looking forward to her night out with her friend Brenda.

Lizzie's mum had told Lizzie to be back to pick up the kids before midday. It was not unusual for her to be late, but when it had gotten to two o'clock her mother had marched the children back home in a temper, expecting to find her still in bed with a hangover.

The back door had been closed but unlocked. There had been no forced entry. She had found Lizzie on the floor dead and had called the police and an ambulance.

She said that she had tried to give mouth to mouth but to no avail. Not surprising as the coroner had said she had been dead for several hours.

Again it had been suffocation with her own pillow. There were no signs of a struggle.

Lizzie had a bite mark on her neck; he'd not been as careful this time, hopefully they would be able to get something from that, dried saliva and Bob's your uncle DNA! They would get the bastard!

Stephen pulled into the station it was five fifteen he had arranged a briefing for six o'clock. As he got out of his car his heart dropped. The press! How the hell had they got information this quick?

He walked towards the entrance head down and pushed his way through the small crowd of vultures who were hungry for a story.

"Detective Roberts, is there any link between this murder and the Jane Smith murder two weeks ago?" shouts one of them.

No reply.

"Detective Roberts do you think this a serial killer?"

Fuck! He thought how the hell had they got hold of that one. If that Paul was anything to do with this he would hang him to dry!

"Detective Roberts have you got any leads?"

No reply.

"Detective Roberts have you any plans to hold a press conference?"

He reached the door, keyed in his security code and shut the door on their ravenous faces, with a sigh of relief.

Just as his heart had stopped pounding the door opened again and Derek dashed in.

"Bloody hell sir, the scavengers are here, who tipped them off?"

"No idea" said Stephen "but I intend to find out!"

He walked though the main office to his office and everyone was in, the place was bustling and everyone was either talking about the murder or on their computers searching for information that may lead them to their man. Well he hoped they were and not surfing on face book, or some other social network site.

What a day, he thought, lounging back in his office chair. He'd phoned Tanya from his mobile after leaving the house. Cancelling another Saturday night, she'd be going off him at this rate and he had phoned the florist to have some flowers delivered.

He attended the briefing at six o'clock and after looking at the basic details, his team shared what they had got.

Paul and Vera had been to see Brenda, she was devastated at the news of her friend's death, sobbed for England, it had taken them a lot of skill and patience to get anything out of her.

They'd had a great night however the evening had ended with Brenda going home alone in a taxi cab and Lizzie in another with a bloke she had been seeing down there and dancing with for the last four weeks. She couldn't remember his name. Ian she thought but couldn't be sure.

Her description of him wasn't much to go on either. About five foot eight, white, brown hair, and medium build aged between thirty and forty.

Lizzie had not said anything about him to her, just that she might be seeing him down there this week.

Nothing at all on what he was wearing; she'd jumped from a blue shirt to a brown shirt, then jeans to trousers.

Bloody hell, Stephen thought that could fit the description of half the men in Leicester.

Vera had looked at all the people they had on computer file that had been arrested in the last ten years with the first name Ian, there had been forty five Ian's. She was happy to follow that up, but didn't hold out much hope, and besides they didn't even know for sure that his name was Ian.

Stephen had spoken to the neighbour, who had maintained to have seen or heard nothing.

Derek and John had spoken to the other neighbours in close vicinity and there was Zilch information there too. They had tracked down the nightclub owner. He was going to speak with his staff and he would get back to them if anyone had any information that might help them.

And that was it. Nothing. The rest of his team had nothing solid either.

"Okay" he said aware that his voice sounded exasperated. Lets brainstorm ideas, see what we can come up with.

"Mind shower, sir" Paul said.

"Mind shower?" Stephen asked trying to see what relevance this had to the case.

"Brainstorm is politically incorrect now sir, so we have to use mind shower"

"Okay" Stephen replied as calmly as he could, incensed at the audacity of this man. They were investigating a fucking murder case for Christ's sake, who the fuck gave a shit.

"Mind storm it is then." He said.

The briefing ended around eight o'clock, nothing of any consequence came out of it, other than the pillow, the pillows in both cases came from the women's bedroom. The murderer would have had to go upstairs to fetch that, how might that have happened.

Lots of ideas were thrown into the pot so to speak, but the consensus was that he could have dosed her with the date rape drug first, then when she was out of it, he could have fetched the pillow then. Not that this led them any closer to the murderer, but it was part of the process, part of the picture building or part of the jigsaw puzzle as Stephen like to call it.

Then it was raised that _if_ she was given a date rape drug and they could only surmise as they hadn't had a toxicology report back yet, however most have them would put money on it, then she wouldn't necessarily take that willingly so he would possibly have spiked her drink.

As it was quick acting, then that would more than likely be done at home rather than the club.

Brenda had said that she was fine when she had left her. So where were the cups or glasses? There was nothing at the scene, that hadn't been checked, so what had they missed? He could have washed it up and put it away.

Ironically it was Paul that had contributed most of these points to the table and they were good points. Very good points Stephen had thought we'll make a good copper out of him yet. He was beginning to use his gut instinct rather than his text books.

Stephen had asked two members of his team to get back to the scene, collect every cup, glass, anything that could be used as a vessel and get them to the lab for the forensic guys. They could have a fingerprint or two on them as well.

They had then looked at the message on the 'calling card.' This had put a smug smirk on Pauls face, Stephen had noticed.

"Another one bites the dust"

One of his team stated that it was a line from a song, sung by the group Queen. He volunteered to download the song and the words to see if there was any hidden message or significance.

Stephen detected that his whole team was motivated to catch this killer and he had left the meeting feeling proud and confident that they would.

Hopefully before he struck again!

Chapter Fifteen

Having spent most of the weekend at the station, Stephen arrived in at around eleven o'clock on Monday morning. The place was quiet, most of his staff was out and about, he guessed.

First thing he needed to do was speak with his chief to update him on the weekends events and how far they had got in the investigation, which needless to say wasn't very far, they were all holding out for the DNA results now, nothing had come from the crockery that the forensic team had spent all weekend on. There had been no traces of any drug, nor were there any fingerprints. Either the perpetrator had worn gloves or had wiped any vessel used.

This killer knew what he was doing; he knew how to avoid detection, but then there was allsorts on the internet now to help people commit the perfect murder, even these criminology courses would describe how to get rid of DNA and what the scenes of crime officers looked for when investigating a crime.

His stomach took a lurch and he repeated back in his mind what he had just thought ......even these criminology courses would describe how to get rid of DNA etc.

Interesting thought, but he couldn't just jump in because of a belief, he had to have evidence and that was in short supply right now.

It didn't stop him thinking about the knowledge Paul had, he had the knowledge of covering up a crime scene and he had the inside knowledge of the investigation and he

135

seemed to know there would be another murder. He could be secretly taunting them, he could be a psychopath and contrary to people's beliefs, there were psychopaths in good jobs, high powered jobs in fact.

He was just contemplating whether to wait until they had the pathology report through before he rang his boss when his telephone on his desk rang.

"Hi Stephen" his boss said raucously but quite jolly, which put Stephen's mind at rest, "hear you've had another busy weekend?"

"Yes Michael" Stephen responded "I was going to call you but I was waiting for the pathologist to ring first, so I could hopefully have some more information for you"

"That's why I'm ringing Stephen." Michael said.

"Owen called less than an hour ago, he'd worked all weekend too, and as you weren't around he spoke to me. So here goes, have you got a pen, if not don't worry he'll fax it over later anyway"

"Fire away Sir, I have a pen" Stephen answered, pen poised attentively listening.

"Death was by suffocation again. Toxicology report reads that she had Rohypnol in her system. And we have some DNA"

He could hear Stephen's sigh of relief. "That's brilliant news sir, was it from the bite"

"No" he replied "she'd had sex, doesn't appear to have been forced sex, so she either did it willingly or he did it to her when she was out for a count, nevertheless, sloppy bastard didn't use a condom!"

"When do we hope to get the DNA results sir?" he asked, hoping this bastard had been arrested in the past.

"Seven to ten days, though they know to rush it through."

Stephen put the phone down both elated and frustrated.

He was happy they had some DNA but frustrated that it would take so long to get the results. He knew that someone would have to sit and go through the database to find a match, but surely there was a simpler system than this.

Maybe they could break the system down into areas, and then they could start by looking in this particular area to find a DNA match, searching further afield if there was not one. It wasn't rocket science for goodness sake!

Never-the-less, in terms of his case at last they might be on to something.

For several years now they had been swabbing anyone that was arrested, even if it was a driving offence, they were building up quite a large DNA data base. He had to accept that it would take time.

He just hoped that this bastard had been arrested for something.

His gut told him that he had, so it was just a waiting game now.

He had been surprised at his boss's joviality they had two murders now and no suspect he would have expected him to be ranting, maybe he was getting calmer in his old age.

He liked Michael, he was sixty and considering retirement, often police officers retired earlier than this, but Michael loved his job too much for that, however he was getting a little slower now and his aches and pains were starting to get to him, he had, had this discussion with Stephen already and he had said that his wife was nagging him to retire and to spend more time with their family.

He and his wife had five children between them and something like eight grandchildren, so he was finding it difficult to keep on working and fulfil his family commitments.

Stephen was secretly pleased as this would mean that he could apply for his job, fill his boots so to speak, and naturally leading the team into action to solve these murders wouldn't do his reputation any harm.

That would be the pinnacle of his career; he didn't need to go any further, he had only ever had his sights on that goal.

And getting a result for these murders would be a bonus.

Chapter Sixteen

Friday 28th March

There was nothing else to do on a Friday night Stephen thought as he washed and shaved.

Tanya was having her usual 'buddy night,' although he had never met any of her friends, as she had never introduced them.

This annoyed him a little, was she ashamed of him, or was she ashamed of them he'd wondered. He'd even thought that she might be seeing a married man that could only get out on a Friday or Sunday night. But quickly squashed that idea out of his head, he couldn't go down that road, it would do his head in.

There again she had never met any of his friends either, maybe she had the same thoughts. Not that he had any friends, but he did have his work colleagues, and it was Bill's fiftieth birthday do, next Saturday. He could take her there, maybe then she would be more open to him meeting her friends sometime.

Bill was the head of the drug squad, they'd known each other since their beat days, and even now with some cases their paths crossed. Drugs and murder were like fish and chips these days.

'Yes' he was pleased with himself; Tanya was a fine looking woman, he would be proud to have her on his arm. He would ask her tomorrow.

He was getting ready to go to Jason's. He might as well have a sniff around, he'd nothing better to do.

They were all still waiting for the DNA results to come through, he had considered getting a few of his team down there tonight, but one they deserved a weekend off and secondly, he didn't want a large police presence at this point as it may drive the murderer underground.

Both girls had been to 'Jason's on the night of their murder his gut instinct told him there was a connection, but even if he learned nothing it filled in some of his time, lonely time, which was time when his thoughts could work overtime about Tanya and what she was doing, those thoughts becoming darker and darker as the evening wore on. He must be getting quite keen on her he contemplated.

He mulled over the last week's events. They'd all listened to the Queen Song over and over again on the stations hi-fi equipment and scrutinised the words of the song, but nothing significant had jumped out at them.

Derek and John had interviewed all of the staff at Jason's and had sat through hours of CCTV, they had followed up a couple of possible leads but had come to a dead end.

Vera had paid visits to most of the 'Ian's' on their data base and they had all had an alibi for one or both of the nights of the murders.

They all felt like they were swimming in mud and getting nowhere. All their eggs were in one basket now the DNA.

He took one more look in the mirror and was pleased with himself, "Handsome chap" he said to himself out loud, "you never know, you may pull tonight, nothing like mixing business with pleasure".

Jason's was a nightclub that was well known for the more mature patrons and for being full of divorcees and single parents, a 'pick up' joint where you were almost certain of getting laid by a single mum 'gagging for it.'

Single mums were quickly getting labelled as easy targets for men, which seemed unfair that a few that gave it up quite easily, should tar the name for many decent single mums but that was how the world worked.

It hadn't helped when the prime minister had recently targeted single parent families as 'dysfunctional families.' He knew as many two parent families that he would deem 'dysfunctional'. Besides his mum had been a single mum to him and his sister and there was nothing dysfunctional about him or his sister.

He found himself a tight spot in the car park, it was full, how many people would be driving home drunk tonight he wondered, then brushed it aside, it wasn't his department and was therefore none of his business.

Jason's was not in the town as most of the clubs in Leicester were it was set back in between field's on the main road between Leicester Forest East and Peckleton.

It was an attractive looking building, and if the Manager had been a little bit more refined it would have made a very nice upmarket restaurant, a successful restaurant as people did not really want to travel into town on a weekend night for a meal, too much trouble in the town centre these days.

It would have brought in a more sophisticated clientele that's for sure.

The queue to get in had only about six people in it, so he stood at the back and waited. He could have shown his warrant card and got straight in, but he didn't want to draw attention to himself, give a possible suspect a head start.

Having paid five pounds to get in he headed for the bar and ordered a coke, he needed to keep his wits about him tonight, he could always have a stiff drink later when he got home.

Coke, lemon and ice in his hand he looked about, bloody hell they were rough in here he thought, covered in tattoos most of them and that were the women.

He noticed a group of rowdy men to his right as he propped up the bar, laughing and joking about something or another.

He eavesdropped for awhile not having much more to do other than observe.

"I came here looking for a lass that's just started her period not someone half way through the fucking menopause" said one laughing out loud, joined boisterously by his companions.

"Not a good looking one in sight" said another

"That women I was dancing with I said to her 'let me make you pregnant, and then you'll be able to get your teeth done on the national health free" this was then followed by more side splitting laughter.

Stephen had, had enough, one reason why he didn't wish to make friends for unruly lad's nights out, he couldn't stand the banter. He easily got offended by the derogatory remarks about women.

Yes he'd be the first to say this place was rough and the women not his type but there was no need to be that offensive. They weren't oil paintings themselves.

He wondered around looking the men up and down rather than the women, he needed to be careful else they'll think I'm a puff, he thought.

It was like looking for a needle in a haystack.

Murderers didn't come in a flasher Mac he pondered like most people think, they weren't ugly men with a axe hidden inside their trench coat. They looked like normal people, and not that this place was full of what he would call 'normal'; it could be anyone of these guys in here.

He didn't know what he was looking for, perhaps someone like him, stood around observing; only Stephen was looking for a prospective suspect and the killer a potential victim.

"Fancy a boogie love" some woman dressed in skin tight leopard pants and a top that barely covered her breasts was looking up at him.

"No thanks, I'm no Fred Astaire" he replied, hoping that would get rid of her. No such luck.

"Well a drink then, mines a vodka and tonic" she purred, trying but not succeeding to look sexy.

"Maybe another time" he said and hastily made a quick retreat.

"Prick" he heard her say as he walked away.

Very appealing, he reflected, wonder what charm school she went to!

Chapter Seventeen

Thankfully no-one else bothered him for the rest of the evening, and he was just about to leave when he saw a face he recognised. He dodged behind a pillar and studied the man stood at the edge of the dance floor.

What the fuck was he doing down here, he questioned. He never said he was coming and I certainly didn't ask him to. He was not down here on police business, so why was he down here?

Stephen stood back, so he couldn't be seen and watched.

Paul was studying people; he seemed to be alone and was totally unaware that he was being watched. Stephen was surprised that Paul hadn't spotted him, but then looked around and saw the crowds around him and understood why. He hadn't noticed the place filling up, too busy people watching, focusing on dubious looking individuals.

Then the same girl that had tried to pull him earlier in the evening had pulled Paul Spencer on to the dance floor and was gyrating her body all over him. He seemed to be enjoying it.

Dark thoughts started to cross Stephens mind again, it was not something that hadn't happened before he thought. Some crime or another had over the years been an inside job.

He then recalled his thoughts the other day ...even these criminology courses would describe how to get rid of DNA etc.

He had brushed them aside, thought he was being irrational and letting his feelings towards Paul get in the way of the investigation, but now he was down here at Jason's without even mentioning it, surely if it was him he wouldn't be that brazen, then he thought but psychopaths were like that, they believed that they were too clever to be caught.

Then his rational mind stepped in, Paul could have come up with the same idea as he had, decided to have a wonder down and sniff about, perhaps he was a sad lonely bastard like he was on a Friday night.

He stood silently observing.

Paul was getting quite into this girl, stroking her hair, kissing her neck. What the hell was going on?

His team were allowed to have a private life of course, but here, why would anyone come here unless they had to, like him. And why hadn't he mentioned that he used this club?

Thoughts streaming through his mind he watched Paul leave the club with the girl in tow, clearly on a promise.

What should I do?

Should I follow him?

He ran these questions through his mind, alongside many more, many more indeed.

He decided in the end not to go after him, he might see him and know that he was onto him if he was the killer or think that Stephen was stalking him if he wasn't.

However, if that girl turned up dead tomorrow he would know just who he would be pointing his finger at!

Stephen eventually walked out into the cold night air and shivered as the icy wind hit him. Blooming weather it was the end of March and still cold enough to snow, he thought.

He hovered around for a while to see if anything of interest happened, anything that appeared to be suspicious, watched as the patrons came out of the club, drunk and boisterous, laughing and playful, some heading for the burger van that was parked outside, greasy food to soak up the drink.

Some of the women were falling over in their high heels unable to walk in them now that they were fuelled with alcohol, skirts pulled up showing their underwear, no dignity he thought.

Then there were those getting into their cars obviously the worse for wear and most definitely over the drink drive limit.

He made a mental note to speak with patrol and get them to monitor this place on a weekend night, rather than focus all their attention on the town centre.

After about half an hour, the cold reaching his bones and nothing irregular to pursue, he got in his car, banged the heating on full blast and drove home to the hum of the warm air floating out of the car radiator.

154

His thoughts drifting back to Paul. He never had liked this guy, not since the day he was transferred to his team. There was something fishy about him. Had his gut been trying to tell him something then? He began to wish that he had followed him but it was too late now.

It was interesting that he knew there would be another murder, what was it he said?

"This is the m.o of a serial killer sir"

Odd, to say that when there had only been one body. None of them had been thinking that this was more than a one off. It was if he was trying to tell them something.

Stephen had put it down to his naivety; he'd thought that he was just being overzealous.

Now his thoughts were much darker, much more sinister. He'd felt for a while that this killer was close to home, he'd not voiced his thoughts, he had no evidence to support this, but they were missing something, he didn't know what but Stephen was sure as hell going to find out!

He pulled up outside his cottage with a plan.

He knew exactly what he was going to do on Monday, but for now he was going to enjoy the rest of his weekend.

Chapter Eighteen

"Fuck me" I nearly got caught, I'm getting far too complacent. I need to be more careful, It made sense that there would be a police presence at Jason's, especially if they had worked out that both of the slag's had been there.

I had been looking around for my next possible victim. I know where most of the girls live. I've been following them home over the last ten months, took notes of their addresses, biding my time. I've watched as they took men in, and seen the bedroom light go on and off within hours of them meeting their prey.

That's what men were to women, their prey, a meal ticket, someone to bring up their spawn and pay the bills whilst they sat around on their big fat arses, drinking coffee all day. They never worked this type; they were the dregs of society, sponged off tax payers. I'm doing the world a favour eliminating them off the face of the earth

I spotted him by chance; hovering around the bar scanning the room, looking for me, no doubt.

He was another one, slept with them, used them for his own satisfaction and then left them to beat up their children and laughed at others misfortunes.

Luckily I managed to hide behind a pillar just as his eyes scanned the place where I had been lurking, his eyes lingering on the spot where I had been standing.

Whoa that was close!

As soon as his eyes lingered somewhere else, I got out of there.

I had a narrow escape, if he'd seen me there he would have unquestionably have came over and spoke to me asked what I was doing there. I'll have to be more careful in the future, let things settle.

I'm home now and safe, but I need to rethink.

****

I guess you want to know more about my mother, everyone does.

You all maintain that you don't want to hear about this stuff,

"Oooh don't tell me anymore" or "I'd rather not hear about it" but you can't help yourself can you?

The curiosity is killing you. Does that make you as sick as me?

Well, turn the page then, go to the next chapter, you don't have to read it.

But you will, won't you,

You just can't help yourself can you?

Everyone's mind is the same as mine you see, you just don't act on it, everyone is capable of bad things even you.

And because you are too cowardly to do what I do, you just enjoy reading about what I do.

You just like intruding on my life, invading my privacy, my private thoughts.

That's fine for now.

I think it might be helpful for me to describe my mother, so you can have a picture in your head; she never leaves mine so why should she not be implanted in yours?

She was not a big woman, quite petite in fact, around five foot and must have only weighed about seven stone, but I was still scared of her, she still petrifies me to this day, even though she's dead, oh yes, she's dead, very dead in fact.

She had a round face with a large thin nose and green eyes. Her hair was long, bleached blonde and always very dry, it reminded me of straw.

When she got up in the morning, mascara caked on her cheeks and stale foundation in blotches she would look like a flippy floppy scarecrow, lolling all over the place, often still drunk from the night before.

She could have been a pretty woman I think, if she'd smiled more, if she hadn't caked all that make up on her face, but she could never have been pretty inside. Inside she was a monster, an evil sadistic fiend.

I was thirteen years old; oh did I forget to tell you, I never went to school, didn't even know there was such a thing as school. In hindsight she probably kept me away so the authorities wouldn't know what was happening to me. I don't know to this day how she managed to evade the establishment, but she did.

Taught me herself................ the harsh way!

Anyway, where was I?

Oh yes I was thirteen years old, by then she'd given up on my education and I now had to work, around the house, you women will know the score, the cleaning, the washing, the ironing and so on.

And by God I had to do it right, but I never did of course, not to her wishes.

I was just putting the vacuum cleaner away when she noticed I'd missed a bit, it was a small blonde hair on her rug.

Well first world war broke out I was battered of course battered almost to death, but that wasn't enough for her, never was enough for her........................

The worst was yet to come!

"The time has come" she said "for you to know the way the world works; you need to know the facts of life son, the birds and the bees"

Well I was thirteen; it was time you may think.

So battered and bruised and still traumatised physically and psychologically, that was when my virginity was broken, that was when I learned about what you mere mortals call lovemaking.....................................

My mother always did reason that practical learning was better than theory.

Chapter Nineteen

Thursday 3rd April

Stephen was sat at his desk doing paperwork and preparing further material that the CPS needed in relation to the up and coming court case of the methamphetamine rapist, as the media were now calling him.

He was also waiting for some information to come through, that he'd been chasing up since Monday.

He'd been looking into Paul Spencer's background after seeing him unauthorised at Jason's on Friday night. Paul had not mentioned to him that he had been down there, and as far as Stephen was aware had not mentioned it to his colleagues either as he had made some discreet enquiries.

There was something bothering him about this guy, and little titbits had been coming through all week, it appeared that Paul had a bit of a dodgy past, he had accumulated a few driving offences, but he had also been under observation in his youth, the police involved at the time could never pin anything on him. So he was curiously waiting for information on why he had been under observation.

There was nothing much doing at the station, no more leads to follow on the two murder cases. They were just sitting ducks, hoping to catch the killer before he struck again.

The atmosphere in the main office was charged, everyone waiting, ready, wanting to do the job they were all paid to do.

The call came direct to Stephen at three fifteen. They'd got a match. They were on the move. Thank god for that Stephen thought, as he thanked his caller and put the phone down, forgetting all about his initial instincts about Paul.

He made a quick call to the control room then he walked into the main office and everyone looked at him in anticipation.

"Right guys, we have a match. The suspects name is Ivan Springer, he is white Caucasian 40 years of age and lives on the Nevington Estate.

Paul see if we can get anything from the DVLA on what vehicle he is currently driving. Vera see if you can find out anything regarding his employment status, Derek, John do some research get anything you can on this man I want us back here ready to roll in.........." he looked at his watch "one hour, that's four thirty precise!"

The place began to buzz, everyone immediately embroiled in their individual tasks, that the time flew by and it only appeared to be five minutes before they were all sat waiting for their boss at four thirty.

Paul had his car type and registration number, which matched what Stephen had obtained from the control room. He had asked them to send a patrol car to cautiously drive by Ivan's home to see if there was a car parked in the vicinity of the house. His car was in his drive, it matched Paul's so therefore the suspect was possibly at home.

Vera had got his social security number and he was currently on unemployment benefits, another probability that he was at home.

Derek and John had pulled up his criminal record status and he had a few minor misdemeanours which were how they had got his DNA on the system.

Stephen gave them their individual responsibilities in the arrest strategy and discussed the plan of action.

By five O'clock they were all on the road to get the man that had fucked up two of their weekends with their families and murdered two innocent girls, and left four children motherless.

****

The arrest went smoothly; Ivan had been in shock and thus had gone quietly and willingly with them into the police car, no kicking and screaming which would have drawn attention to the arrest and subsequently brought the press sniffing around the station wanting a piece of the action, hankering after a news story confirming that the killer was now being held and questioned.

Ivan had been processed in the arrest suite and they were just waiting for the duty solicitor to arrive, which he had requested, so that they could begin their interrogation.

Stephen had decided that Derek and John would be the best men for this task and was just about to speak with them when Paul knocked on his door.

"Yes Paul" he said as he looked up into the face of the man that he once believed was a suspect.

"I was wondering sir" Paul said "if I could be part of the interrogation. I have the skills sir and would like to gain a bit more experience"

This was a fucking double murder case Stephen thought, did he really think that he was going to allow him to do his 'skills practice' on this one!

"No, Paul, not this time, I will bear you in mind when something else comes up though" Stephen said lowering his head back down to his paperwork, letting Paul know that he was being dismissed.

"But sir, I think I...................." Paul was not going to give up that easily.

"Look Paul" Stephen snapped "Derek and John will be handling this one. There is only one way to unfold a note, without tearing the paper and they know how to do it, if you get my meaning" and to ensure that Paul left the office without any further 'buts' he got up from his desk and held the door, ready to shut it when he sulkily left.

****

The tape whirling in the background, Derek stated the usual procedure for suspect interviews:

This interview will be taped...................

Ivan nodded looking anxiously at the duty solicitor as he did so.

He hadn't felt very confident with him and had noticed that he appeared irritated that he had been pulled away from whatever he was doing. He had spent five minutes maximum with him before the interview and had said very little to reassure him.

Ivan felt scared, very scared.

"Would you like to start by telling us about the evening of Friday 21st March into the early hours of Saturday 22nd March" Derek asked.

"What from beginning to end"

"Yes"

"Well I had a birthday party starting at seven o'clock with one of my friends from this transvestite group that I am a part of, so I went there, then I left about nine to go home and quickly get changed because I had promised to meet Lizzie at Jason's"

"Get changed?" Derek asked, not understanding why he had to get changed.

"Yes, I was in drag you see, dressed as a woman, Lizzie doesn't know about..... about my other life"

"Okay"

"I had planned to meet Lizzie and didn't want to let her down and..."

171

"How long had you known Lizzie? Derek asked.

"About four weeks, we'd been chatting and dancing and things, you know"

"And so on Friday 21st you met her down Jason's is that right? Then what happened?" Derek asked.

"We chatted and danced for a while, then we er... got a taxi and went back to her house"

"Had you been to her house before?"

"No" Ivan replied "This was the first time.

"And then what?" Derek asked.

"We had sex" Ivan replied.

Derek looked at John and they both knew that they had to tread carefully here; this guy could get away with this if they didn't. Clever bastard had worked out that they had DNA so was covering himself by admitting that they had sex.

172

"Was the sex good?" It was John's turn now and Derek had worked with him long enough to know where this was heading.

"What?" Ivan asked.

"Was the sex good?" John asked again "Did she enjoy it?"

"I er think so" Ivan replied confused by this line of questioning.

"What time did you leave?" John asked.

"Oh, after about half an hour" Ivan replied pleased that this uncomfortable subject had been dropped. "She made me a potted beef sandwich then said she was tired"

"So" John said "in the space of half an hour, you entered the house, performed foreplay, had sex and then she made you a potted beef sandwich and I'm guessing you ate it, did you have drink with that?"

"Yes, a cup of tea"

"So how long exactly did the foreplay and sex last Ivan, two, minutes?"

"I don't know I didn't time it?" Ivan replied, his face starting to flush.

"She can't have been very happy Ivan, what happened next did she taunt you, accuse you of being a lousy lover?"

"No!" Ivan replied looking at his solicitor, wasn't he supposed to fucking do something here, he thought.

"Is that why you killed her Ivan, did she ridicule you, damage your male ego?"

"No!" Ivan replied

"Of course she didn't, we know that Ivan, you know that too, don't you?"

"Yes" Ivan replied.

"I believe you Ivan, I believe you're telling the truth, we all know that she didn't taunt you" and just as the relief was spreading across Ivan's face, John jumped in with his ace card.

"She couldn't ridicule you because she was out for the count wasn't she? Because you'd spiked her with a date rape drug hadn't you?!" John shouted.

Ivan sat there with this mouth wide open, he couldn't respond, these guys really thought he had hurt Lizzie, even his solicitor must do because he had not helped him one little bit.

"Interview terminated at" Derek looked at his watch "9 p.m."

He switched off the tape and both he and John left the room without saying another word.

"We'll leave him to sweat on that for a bit" John said to Derek as they left the interview room and were out of earshot.

"Let's go and see what they have turned up at his house, or in his belongings," and they headed to the evidence room. This would be where anything of interest taken from Ivan's home, car etc would have been bagged up and stored.

Chapter Twenty

It was ten o'clock when Derek and John knocked on Stephens door, he had been waiting for them to get a run down on their progress before he headed home.

"Come on in lads" he responded "anything to report."

"Well we've left him sweating sir, he's admitted to having sex with her. I think he'll crack sir, he's pretty bloody nervous." Derek said.

John handed him two evidence bags. Stephen looked at the first one; it contained a small clear glassed bottle containing a yellow liquid.

"What's this?" he asked "Don't know sir we're about to send it to the lab, but thought you should see it first."

"Erm interesting" he said picking up the second bag.

His heart suddenly went cold; he could feel his face going ten shades whiter than white and his hands beginning to shake. He must stay calm he thought.

In his hands in a clear plastic bag was a business card and written in bold letters was:

Tanya Wright – Psychosexual therapist

John broke into his thoughts, clearly not noticing Stephens's anxiety,

"We thought we'd take this in and ask him about it, might be something to it, having a sex therapist's card and this being a potential sex motivated crime"

"Yes, yes," Stephen answered trying not to sound too interested.

"Let me know what he says, then wrap it up for tonight, let him sleep on things and we will re interview him in the morning. Thanks guys" he said desperately wanting them out of his office before they noticed his distracted and concerned behaviour.

****

Derek and John re-entered the interview room, re did the tape procedure and Derek put the card in front of him and asked

"You had this card in your belongings, can you tell us who it is and why you have it?"

"No problem, it's my therapist Tanya, I've been seeing her for about two years"

"What for" Derek asked.

"For my problem, my cross dressing"

It was Johns turn now to intervene.

"Two years of therapy for cross dressing?"

"Well not just that, there were other things"

"Like what" John asked.

"Well my sex life things like that"

"Like what?" Derek now piped in.

"Oh bloody hell do I have to go into that"

"It's important that we know everything Ivan, for all we know this woman may be next on your list" Derek answered "And it could actually help your case, prevent you from being charged" he lied using his I'm your best friend tactic.

"For what I've already told you I haven't done anything" he shouted and then hastily calmed down, knowing that shouting would not go in his favour, not with these bastards they were trying to mess with his head. They were trying to bloody set him up and his solicitor had clearly gone to fucking sleep. He needed to stay focused.

"Okay, okay," he said containing his anger. "I have a sex problem, an erection problem"

"You didn't appear to have that problem the night you met Lizzie"

"No I'm okay if I'm not emotionally involved, and we talked about my mother sometimes too" he added keen to get off the subject of his sex life.

"What about your mother"

"She was domineering, suffocated me"

"She suffocated you" John seized upon this and again Derek knew where he was going with it.

"Yes"

"Interesting that"

"What?"

"That she suffocated you" John replied a grin crossing the whole of his face.

"Well she did" Ivan said morosely

"Just like you suffocated Jane and Lizzie" he said.

"Interview terminated at" Derek looked at his watch, "eleven fifteen"

They both left the room, leaving both Ivan and his solicitor dumbfounded.

****

It was midnight by the time Stephen got in his car to drive home, his thoughts in turmoil.

Tanya, his girlfriend was the suspect's therapist. They were going to Bill's party on Saturday night, where most of his team would be. He would have to introduce her; they would then put two and two together.

It would be unethical for him to not say anything and this unnerved him. He liked to keep his private life, private.

As far as he could see he could not pull out of taking her, this would upset her and leave her feeling that he was ashamed of her. He could find an excuse not to go himself or he could be upfront with his team. Both options left him feeling tense.

Stephen was feeling drained. This whole case was getting to him. He decided that he was best to sleep on it, and make a decision in the morning.

****

Ivan sat in the cells rubbing his forehead, sweat dripping onto the grubby wooden table. It was five o'clock on Friday. They had held him for almost twenty four hours now and a decision had to be made. He had not admitted anything during the interrogation that they could clearly use as a confession. All they had was the DNA and the dental match to Lizzie's bite mark.

He had admitted having sex with her and to biting her but adamantly denied murdering her.

Stephen and Derek watched him through the two way mirror as he picked his nose and flicked it on the floor.

"What do you think sir" Derek asked, trying not to think about what he had just seen for fear of heaving.

"He's not gonna crack, sure a tough one this one, especially for a tranny, we've got the DNA and the dental match that's all we need to charge him, he was the last person to see Lizzie alive, so that's enough for me." Stephen said. "Charge him Derek and then get yourself home, it's been a long couple of days."

His boss left the room and relieved to be going home, Derek went to look for John so that they could nail this bastard do the paperwork and get the hell out of there. It had been a long week.

Stephen left the station still feeling unsettled. He had decided to take Tanya to the party on Saturday and had called his team together to disclose his relationship with the suspect's therapist. It had been a difficult decision and one that he had spent most of the night tossing and turning over.

However he had always tried to be honest with his team and honesty had been the best policy in this case.

Besides he had listened to his gut and his gut had told him to come clean, and as he always said his gut was always right!

Chapter Twenty-One

Saturday 5th April

Tanya was a psychosexual therapist had been for about ten years now and loved her job immensely.

She had her own private practice and got most of her work through self referral and multi agencies, which sometimes the client paid for and occasionally agencies paid for. She was building up a very reputable reputation and becoming a well respected therapist in not only the Leicester area, but further afield.

She'd even recently had a book published that she had written about sex therapy, the process and the variations in client work. She'd included some of the underlying issues to client's sex problems, techniques that therapists could use when working with this particular client group and how to manage their own personal transference that was inevitable when working with sexual issues. She had then finished it off with some theory on transsexual and transgender issues. It was selling well and she was very proud of herself.

Most people believed that it must affect your sex life doing a job like hers but it didn't, she was able to switch off from the stories that she heard on a daily basis as soon as she shut the door of her upmarket therapy room, each day.

Switched off she was tonight, it was Saturday night and that was her and Stephen's night.

Now was the time to concentrate on her own sex life.

She liked Stephen but didn't love him, she could never marry she'd known that since she was twenty one years old. It would mean that she would have to share her secret and no way was she going to do that. Not a cat in hells chance, she would carry that to her grave.

Stephen was twenty years older than her, but that didn't matter to Tanya. Why people worried about age she never knew, it was about two people wanting to be together, that was what was important. She'd always preferred older men, made up for the father she never had she supposed, but hey ho, that was something she would have to work out in her own therapy, if she ever got round to having any.

Tanya was getting ready in her bedroom he would be round soon and she wanted to look good for him, she loved dressing up.

She could do any look really when she put her mind to it. She could dress classy, professional, elegant, stylish, chic and even a tasteful tart if she was in the right mood.

She was just sipping back the dregs of her wine when the news came on the television. They had charged a guy with Jane Smith and Lizzie Benton's murder; she froze as she saw the killer's picture come up on to the screen.

"Oh my God" she exclaimed out loud, her thoughts rushing around like ants marching through her head. How can that be?

Ivan Springer, was a client of hers, had been for about two years now. He was a pleasant enough guy, a transvestite who struggled to maintain a serious relationship due to his clandestine life.

He could never manage to keep his need to dress as a woman hidden very long. His yearning was far too frequent for it to be kept concealed.

Ivan had originally engaged in therapy because this was affecting all of his relationships and wanted to be what he perceived to be 'normal', however more recently they had been discussing how it was getting more and more difficult for him to maintain an erection unless he was dressed as a woman.

He'd disclosed that he could manage it okay with one night stands, although he had found that on those occasions he had ejaculated too soon, but this didn't bother him. The problem arose so to speak if he became emotionally involved.

Tanya had discussed with him how it may be more about attachment then his need to dress as a woman.

They had also gone on to process his relationship with his powerful and engulfing mother and the impact that this had on him now in his relationships with women. Ivan was just beginning to come to an awareness of how his history impacted on his present and they were reaching a crucial part of his therapy where the unconscious was becoming more conscious and was likely to facilitate change.

Tanya was dumbfounded. He was such a nice man, a gentle person, not capable of harming a fly, let alone a double murder.

What should she say to Stephen? Should she say anything she wondered?

Then her heart did another triple jump! He probably knew. He'd telephoned her earlier and arranged to pick her up sooner than they had initially planned. Perhaps this is why; perhaps he wanted to talk with her first.

He had sounded a little off she thought or was she just being paranoid?

She poured herself another glass of wine and attempted to calm herself down, this is just wonky thinking, she thought, he might not know and even if he did there was nothing wrong with that. He must know that she couldn't say anything due to patient/therapist confidentiality.

She looked in the mirror and admired herself, putting her irrational thoughts behind her.

She did look good tonight, she'd wanted to, if she was meeting Stephen's friends and often when you want to look particularly good, something would go wrong, the make-up or the hair, her stomach would bloat or something. But no, tonight she looked exceptionally good. He would be proud of her.

****

It was seven fifteen and Stephen was on his way to pick up Tanya, he'd contemplated not saying anything about Ivan Springer, he hadn't wanted to spoil the night and besides they never discussed each other's work, but he'd established that he'd had no choice.

Someone was bound to say something tonight, make some comment and then she would be confused and possibly embarrassed and he didn't want to put her through that.

So, he had rang her and arranged to see her earlier than planned. They could have a glass of wine; he could discuss this new element to his case, put it to bed and enjoy the rest of their night.

He arrived at her door at seven thirty precise, pleased with himself for being on time. He rang the doorbell and took a step back in surprise when she opened the door. She looked absolutely stunning, more striking than he'd ever seen her. She had gone to a lot of trouble tonight and he was pleased.

She handed him a glass of wine and they both sank down into her feather filled sofa looking at each other, admiring the effort that they had both gone to.

Tanya spoke first.

"How's things?" she asked, feeling nervous at what this might have instigated.

Stephen decided to come straight to the point, get it out of the way.

"We arrested a guy called Ivan, Ivan Springer today" he said watching her face for a reaction, and mildly disappointed that there was not one.

"Did you?" she replied.

"Yes, apparently he is one of your clients"

"Is he?" she again gave a non-committed response.

He hated it when she answered a question with a question. This was something he'd noticed she always did when he asked her anything that may be slightly intruding on her personal life.

"Tanya, you must know who your clients are, he's been seeing you for two years for goodness sake!" he said not able to contain his irritation.

"And you must know Stephen" she replied calmly "that I can't even tell you whether this man you have a arrested is a client, let alone anything about him, so it might be a good idea to change the subject don't you think?"

Another bloody question, he thought. She could be so infuriating at times. But she looked so beautiful tonight; he couldn't stay angry for long and decided that it was best put to bed.

He'd known she was professional and would not break client confidentiality, and he had just wanted to pre-warn her in case something was said tonight, so no point dragging it out.

"I know, I guess I just wanted to warn you really in case any of the lawyers, defence or prosecution, wanted to speak to you. Anyway" he quickly changed the subject "let's go and grab something nice to eat then go to this party. I am looking forward to showing you off. You look absolutely stunning tonight Tanya, did I tell you that?"

"No you didn't" she smiled trying to hide the fear that she was now feeling inside.

****

It was midnight and Tanya and Stephen had just arrived home from the party. It had been a good night, everyone had struggled to keep their eyes off Tanya, Stephen had noticed, not surprising she looked beautiful. They were probably well jealous that he had such a beautiful woman. She could hold good conversations too, about anything that people talked to her about; she was intellectual and a bloody good listener. He had felt so proud.

He had learned a lot more about Tanya tonight too, seeing her in the company of others and he was very impressed.

I could fall for this woman he thought and quickly discounted that notion as the drink altering his very determined mind that love was not on the cards for him and never would be.

Tanya came into her dimly lit living room then interrupting his thoughts. She was wearing a lilac negligee that clung to her bosom figure, immediately giving him an erection. She was beautiful, and downright sexy he thought as she took his hand and led him into her bedroom

****

"How do you do that he asked?" as they were lying entwined in each other's arms having made the most passionate love he had ever experienced.

"Do what?" she asked running her French polished fingernails through his chest hair.

"Enjoy sex as much as you do, when you work with sex all day long?" he asked.

"How do you when you work with murders all day long?" she asked.

Answering another question with a question he thought.

When would she ever show just a little bit of herself?

When would she let him inside her head?

What was she hiding of herself?

They both then fell into a contented sleep.

<u>Chapter Twenty-Two</u>

Saturday 5th April

Paul was spitting nails tonight, ready to kill! It was ten o'clock and he'd just arrived home from Bill's party.

"If that fucking prick humiliates me again I swear I will deck him" he said aloud, pacing his flat like a demented lunatic.

"Fucking prancing about with his posh tart, like he was someone special, and showing me up yet again!" he raged.

Stephen had introduced his team to Tanya, his girlfriend, who was Paul, had to admit a bit of a stunner, lord knows how that Pratt had managed to pull her.

He had introduced all the other guys in a pleasant way but when he had got to Paul he had said.

"This is Paul aka Cracker, our criminal profiler" he had laughed, and all the lads had burst out laughing in unison.

He had taken the piss out of him again, he constantly undermined his skills, didn't take anything he said seriously, treated him like the office idiot!

The only one that hadn't laughed was Vera, she had caught sight of Pauls face and seen the impact those words had on him and had looked away with uneasiness. She had even endeavoured to console him later on in the evening, told him not to take it to heart, but Paul was inconsolable and left early before he did something that he might regret.

He had thought about it, he'd thought about going up and punching the fucker on the nose, showing him up in front of his girlfriend, the girlfriend who incidentally was the therapist to our current murder suspect.

She was a sex therapist at that, he had kept that quiet. How had he met her, probably accessing treatment himself?

She was all smiles and flowery talk, she wasn't miss sweetie pie he could tell, probably had sex with her clients to show them how it should be done. Hope she gave him a dose of the clap!

He had still been fuming about Stephen's comment on Thursday when he'd asked to interview the suspect, covertly suggested that he would make a fuck up of it, and then letting bloody Laurel and Hardy do the deed. Now this, Stephen had added fuel to an already burning fire, now he would pay. Paul didn't know how or when but what he did believe in was Karma and he felt sure that Karma would come through.

He believed that in the end Karma would catch him up and dish him right back all that he has dished out to others, and when it did Paul would laugh.

Derek and John, or Laurel and Hardy as he liked to call them, hadn't done much better, they hadn't got a confession out of the suspect, but rather than admit that this was probably because he was innocent, they think he's clever and covering his back.

They were just a pair of bully boys, who manipulated suspects, twisted their words to fit the crime and then boasted about it in the office afterwards. There was probably many an innocent man doing time in prison due to their handy work. And any dumb fool could see that this man is innocent.

"They just ain't got a fucking clue" he laughed "sent that bottle away to the lab for testing; all the twats had to do was smell it. They were time and money wasters and complete wastes of space." He was talking to himself now, something he had started to do since he began living alone particularly when he was mad.

Paul had gone into the station that morning and got an update on the recent events. He had already been to the evidence room the day before and took a whiff of the liquid in the bottle.

It was liquid nitrogen otherwise known as 'poppers,' it had gone straight to his head as soon as he had smelt it and he'd known straight away what it was from his drug taking days. But no-one had asked for his opinion, so he wasn't going to give it!

They had thought it might be Rohypnol, for fucks sake how thick are they? Rohypnol is a small white tablet with no taste or odor. They only had to bleeding Google it for Christ's sake. But no they'd sent it to the lab at a cost of lord knows what to have it tested. Money was tight anyway, they had to buy their own pens because there was never any in the stationary cupboard and they were wasting their precious resources like this.

They really do deserve a pat on the head he thought….. With a fucking shovel!

And the fucking twats have now arrested and charged the wrong man, they were too quick to make an arrest, score points, they hadn't thought things through.

Not like he had.

Serial killers were psychopaths, and psychopaths didn't go into therapy.

Psychotherapy, involved trust and a relationship with the therapist, this was out of the question, because psychopaths were incapable of opening up to people, let alone a therapist.

Also they don't want to change, don't think they need to change, and even he knew that therapy was primarily about change.

Psychopaths were incapable of having meaningful relationships, they view others as fodder for manipulation and exploitation and this guy Ivan, was in therapy trying to improve his relationships with women.

And last but not least psychopaths are diagnosed by their purposeless and irrational antisocial behavior, their lack of conscience, and emotional vacuity. They were thrill seekers, literally fearless. They were impulsive by nature and fearless of the consequences.

This guy Ivan was not demonstrating any of these behaviors', he had not got any previous convictions for anti social behaviors', he'd had a bar fight and a measly driving offence that was all, and ironically psychopaths are a great success with the ladies. This guy was having therapy because of his lack of success with the ladies.

The whole team were just gullible fools; they listened to and acted on everything Stephen fucking Roberts said. They hadn't got an ounce of psychological awareness between them.

"Gut instinct!" that's what he had said on more than one occasion. They had to rely on their gut instinct. Did they not know that they had to use their head too, their mind, their brains.

If they had any brains, there was not a decent brain cell between the lot of them he concurred.

Paul rolled a joint; he needed something to calm him down. He would need several tonight the mood he was in.

He took a long deep drag of the cannabis packed cigarette and settled back in his chair. This man was a massive trigger for his drug use; he was smoking more now than he ever did.

He closed his eyes and made a sensible decision.

He was going to have to solve this case by himself, he realized this now. He couldn't rely on anyone on that team, not even Vera although she was the brightest, she was a people pleaser and would follow the majority and he was unmistakably the minority. So it was down to him and him alone.

They had arrested the wrong man, he was even more certain of that, than he was anything.

This meant of course that there would without any doubt be another murder, and he was going to try and prevent that. He wasn't sure how or when, but he would.

Paul fell into a contented sleep induced by the depressant he was now becoming more and more dependent on.

Chapter Twenty-Three

Bloody stupid that's what they are, they've arrested the wrong bloody man, not that I hoped they'd arrest me but I wanted that 'prick' to know who I am, know what this was about.

Why not? He wouldn't recognise me now anyway, I've changed. No he'd never know me now, not in a million years. Well he knows me sort of, but he doesn't really know me.

But we'll see when I give a little clue next time. I planned it on the third and so I will do it on the third.

Gut Instinct

Do you wanna know?

What the clue is?

I bet you do, don't you.

Curiosity killed the cat, and I'm Curiosity you know........................ and you're the fucking Cat!

Bet you're worried now. I bet you're shaking in your boots.

Is it dark outside? It is isn't it?

Have you looked out your window?

Go on,

You could be my next victim!

I'm watching you...

Gotcha! ☺

Well enough of my silly games, let's get serious.

'God gives every bird a worm, but he does not throw it into the nest"

Gut Instinct

You'll have to work that one out for yourself like he will.

My life is so much better now that I am in control. I was so out of control when I was a kid.

I'll tell you now of the worst thing that she ever did to me,

I don't want you to feel sorry for me, but I would like you to understand why I have done some of the things that I have done.

It was worse than any of the sexual or physical abuse, it was when I realised that one day I would kill her, over, and over and over again.

I was ten years old, maybe eleven. We were sat watching the television, she was drinking as usual, and I was fetching and carrying as usual.

"Get me another drink dickhead"

"Fetch me a biscuit twat face"

"Go and have a piss for me Son!"

I sat trying to work out how I was going to do that, I thought she meant it and I was about to get up and do it. Or try to at least, until she laughed out loud, that croaky laugh that ended up with her coughing her guts up from all the fags that she smoked.

We were watching a documentary on television. It was about all these young children that had been abducted from their parents, on parks, beaches, and back gardens.

Their mothers had only taken their eyes off them for a minute, and whoosh they were gone, never to be seen again. The mothers devastated and talking on the television, wondering what they looked like now at sixteen, nineteen, twenty five.

I remember thinking I wish someone had done that to me, but fat chance I'd never been out the house, since that day at the park, never even been in the garden, not that anyone would see me if I had, the grass had always been overgrown, five or six feet high.

Gut Instinct

If I'd been abducted I would have had a better life, anything was better than this.

Once the credits rolled and the programme was over, my mother looked at me sadly, she hadn't done that before, she'd never looked at me sadly, only ever looked at me with contempt.

Then she said it, it was then she gave me a shred of hope:

"That happened to you son, I abducted you"

"When, from where" I asked.

"Fetch us another drink and then I'll tell you, no second thoughts fetch us the bloody bottle"

I rushed into the kitchen and got her what she had asked. I was not hers I had another mother somewhere, a mother that was probably looking for me.

I felt elated. I could visualise my impending freedom. I could almost sense the strength of my real mother's arms around me, the warmth of her tears falling on to my cheeks. I could feel her undying love oozing into my wounds, her soft hands touching them and healing them.

I poured her a drink and gave her the bottle. Glaring at her waiting, knowing that she would only speak when she was ready and if I asked too many questions, she would shut down completely.

And then she told me,

"Well son when you was about one, I was looking for a child, I couldn't have them you see, I had an illness when I was younger that made me infertile.

I was a cleaner for people with money, lots of money at the time.

One day as I was walking home from work, I saw you, playing in the garden of this lovely house, with swings and slides and a swimming pool in the garden.

I stood and watched you for a while and your mummy came out, she was the most beautiful woman I had ever seen. Not fair that, not fair that some women should have it all, beauty, money, nice house, children, handsome husband. I remember thinking that at the time, not fair that she should have everything and I should have nothing.

I watched you playing contentedly with all these wonderful toys, and her looking at you with love in her eyes, and then she turned and went inside.

That's when I did it! I snatched you, ran away with you and kept you for myself"

I could feel the tears welling up in my eyes, not from sadness, from happiness. I had another mummy, a better mummy, a mummy that was out there looking for me.

"Off to bed now son" she said serious and deep in thought.

I hopped, skipped and jumped up those stairs feeling happier than I ever had.

For the next two weeks I lay awake waiting, waiting for her to find me, to come and get me. I dreamed the most picturesque and exquisite dreams of my mother, my home and the wonderful life that I would have, once I was found.

Then in my dark moments I would figure out how unrealistic this was. How would she ever find me, no-one even knew I existed.

My mother had never mentioned it again, and I knew better than to ask.

That's when I came up with my plan, if Mohammed couldn't come to the mountain, if my mummy couldn't come to me then the mountain would go to her.

I waited tolerantly until Friday night came when I knew she would be out the house from seven thirty until eleven thirty. I'd never done this before and knew the consequences of my actions would be catastrophic if I was to be caught. But I didn't care, I had something to cling on to now, I had the promise of another life, a better life.

Friday night came and I watched her get ready, dancing around the kitchen in an animated way, as she always did on a Friday night, made up like a clown, skirts just below the knicker line and tops just above the nipple.

I was energised today too. Today I was going to find who my real mother was then I was going to run away and find her.

It was hard to keep my excitement contained, but I did, I was a good actor, I'd learned from one of the best.

As soon as she left I was up on my feet and headed for my destination, her room.

My mother was a narcissist you see, if there had been any media coverage about me, she would have kept it, it would have thrilled her, and gained her some kind of covert negative attention.

I knew she kept all her personal stuff in her wardrobe, so I took one box out after another, there were old photographs of a child, her I assumed, with stern looking adults, her parents maybe.

I rummaged through old bills and old bank statements and memorabilia from her schooldays. There was a newspaper cutting of her when she was in her teens describing her as a bit of a tearaway and uproar that as part of her punishment she was going to be sent to a holiday camp.

There were some old love letters from a guy she had been writing to in prison eight years ago.

Minutes passed into hours until all these boxes of what to me was rubbish lay spewed all over the bedroom floor.

Nothing! I felt so disheartened. I was sure I would find something here. But eternal optimist that I am, I didn't stop, I emptied her drawers of all her clothes searching, hoping and then I found it, a locked old wooden box in the bottom drawer of her tall boy. Yes this was where she would keep her most hidden secrets.

I ran downstairs two steps at a time and got a kitchen knife and ran back to the bedroom almost wetting my pants with anticipation and I broke open the box, all of its contents falling on to the floor, fumbling through them like there was no tomorrow.

Then I found it, there would be no tomorrow..........................

In my hands lay my birth certificate with her name down as my mother.

She had lied........ she had fucking lied.

I sat on the floor that night in the midst of all that mess and I cried, and cried and cried.

I picked up a lighter off her bedside table and I set light to my birth certificate and watched it burn.

I was still crying and watching the flames turn my birth certificate into ashes and spread to the other papers on the floor, when I heard her come home and climb the stairs with her next conquest. I didn't care, my life was over anyway.

I still recall the look on her face when she came into the bedroom, and I still recall the consequences of my actions.

This is when I developed an interest in fire.

Chapter Twenty-Four

Thursday 10th April

Tanya was on the Leicester to Birmingham train, it was extremely busy she was lucky to get a seat, just managed to grab one with a table near the window. She had spent most of the journey gazing out of the window deep in thought as the trees and houses whizzed by.

She hadn't told Stephen that she was coming to Birmingham. She didn't know what he would say, how he would react and most of all she did not want the interrogation when she got back.

She had been totally surprised to get the visiting order and the desperate letter from Ivan for her to visit. She'd contemplated not going but the curiosity would have killed her, she hated being out of control, the not knowing would have been worse. She wanted to know what he wanted. She needed to know if his defence team were going to try and use her.

"The next stop will be Birmingham New Street" came over the train's tannoy system. She grabbed her bag and waited for the train to slow down as it was entering the station.

She needed to then get to Winson Green Prison where Ivan was being held on remand. She was feeling anxious, she had never been to a prison before and didn't relish the idea of it now, didn't know what to do when she got there, what the procedure was and how she would feel.

She had spent most of last night lying awake, going through the conversations that they may have so that she had prepared answers. She would rather have this conversation with him now to prevent any surprise subpoenas. If that happened, God she couldn't bear thinking about that, the truth would undoubtedly come out.

She recalled a client telling her about his experience in court. He had been trying to claim compensation for an accident he'd had at work. He was faking it and he'd been comfortable disclosing that to her knowing that their sessions were confidential.

He was claiming that the accident had damaged his right leg to a point where he could hardly use it.

The whole case went up in flames when the employer's barristers produced an application form that he had filled in four weeks previously for a job as a bus driver, where they hastened to add that he would have to use his right leg quite a lot for this line of employment.

He'd been gob smacked, couldn't understand how they had got hold of this material, and even more dumbfounded when the judge ordered him to pay court costs which amounted to more than his compensation claim would have been.

This was a double murder case, there would be even more scrutiny, more need to discredit witnesses from either side.

The barristers would have a field day if they looked into her background.

NO this could not happen, she would move away before she would step foot in a court of law.

The train slowly pulled into the station and she pushed through the crowds that were trying to get on as she was getting off, why they can't just wait until we've got off she thought, exasperated by the ignorance of people.

Birmingham was busy, people rushing about reminiscent of an ant colony, shoving and pushing to get to their own destinations no consideration for anyone else.

She hailed a taxi and asked for Winson Green Prison.

Thirty minutes later, a journey that should have only taken ten if it wasn't for all the traffic, and she was outside the prison.

It was a tall green building surrounded unsurprisingly by a tall brick wall. It was a hideous building and should be she supposed, it must house some quite unpleasant people.

She entered the building and was told by a miserable looking screw to go over the road to a building that looked not dissimilar to a community centre. Apparently she had to book in there first, she'd be given a number then when her number was called she would come back over to the prison.

It felt like a daft system but hey ho who was she to say.

The area was pretty scary she thought lots of odd looking characters hanging around or stood doing what looked like deals on the corner. She held her handbag close to her and crossed the road,

When she walked into the building it was jam-packed with women, a few men and what seemed like hundreds of kids all running riot.

She walked up to the counter and handed the woman her visiting order.

"You need to hang on to that love" she said "take it across with you, here's your number 98, you are"

"How long will I have to wait" Tanya asked, not relishing the idea of hanging around here all afternoon.

"How longs a piece of string" she said, then noticing Tanya's downfallen face she said

"Shouldn't be no longer than about an hour and a half love, take a seat if you can find one, grab yourself a cuppa, and if you need any support there's a lady over there at that desk who can tell prisoners wives what they are entitled to, I can tell you're a new one."

Tanya couldn't be bothered to correct her, she contemplated going out for a walk for half an hour but she didn't know which appeared more terrifying in here or outside.

She got herself a cup of coffee and by chance found herself a seat at a table on her own. The noise was excruciating to her ears, she looked around at the people waiting patiently for their number to be called.

How ironic Tanya thought all the prisoners were numbers and the prisoners wives or family were too by all accounts. She and everyone in this room were just a number visiting a number. Not such a bad thing for her though she mused.

She sat looking around wishing she had brought a magazine or something, not wanting to open herself out to conversation or inquisitive questions.

The way some of the women dressed was startling, looked more suited to a street corner with a five pound note pinned to their arses Tanya thought.

She scolded herself, she was not usually this judgemental but she couldn't see the point in them dressing in this way. What were they trying to do tease their men with something they could not have?

She'd been there over an hour when she noticed one woman hit her kid so hard he fell off the chair, it took Tanya all her strength not to go over and say something, she hated to see children treated in this way.

"Numbers eighty five to 100 please" a prison officer had come into the room and she was saved from her actions.

That was her. She got up and they all followed the officer over the road, in line like school children on a school trip.

She followed the others and handed her visiting order in, then waited to be escorted to the visitor's room.

God she would be glad when this day was over, and she would never visit a prison again, she knew that for certain. It was the most demoralising situation she had ever been in.

Chapter Twenty-Five

When she entered the visitor's room she scoured the tables for Ivan. They all looked the same in their blue jeans, blue striped shirts and pale faces from having no sun. The only difference was that some of them had a yellow band across their shoulder.

Then she saw him, stood up waving. She walked over noticing other women kissing and hugging their loved ones and being told to sit down by the screws.

Ivan shook her hand and thanked her for coming. They sat in silence for what seemed like an age, neither of them knowing what to say. Tanya broke the silence first.

"How are you?" she asked

"I didn't do it Tanya, you know that don't you?" answering her question with a question.

"What's the yellow stripe for" she asked not quite wanting to commit herself.

"That's put on prisoners that are an escape or suicide risk" he replied.

"Oh," she said.

Silence again. This time Ivan broke the silence.

"They're saying I killed two women Tanya and I didn't, my brief says I'm looking at life if they find me guilty." He pleaded, tears forming in his eyes

"He's suggested I do a plea, but I've said no, I'm not going down for something I didn't do"

"No, no that would be wrong" was all Tanya could say.

"So, I need all the help I can get"

"Yes, yes I'm sure you do"

"So I was thinking" he said. Here it comes Tanya thought, what I was expecting and what I've prepared for. I'd just hoped I wouldn't have to do this.

"Thinking what?" She asked biding herself some time.

"Will you give evidence for me, Tanya? I think it might help, you know"

"In what way Ivan?" she asked.

"Well, you've been working with me; you can tell them that I haven't done it!"

"Ivan" Tanya said calmly. "As much as I believe you, I don't know that you didn't do it....."

"But............." Ivan interrupted.

"Let me finish Ivan" Tanya said. "Of course, I would like to help you, but I don't think me giving evidence would go in your favour"

"Why" Ivan asked concern etched on his face.

"Because if I stood in court, I would possibly have to give information that you have disclosed to me"

"Yes well that's fine" he said "I have no problem with that, I will sign to say that you can"

"Ivan, you don't understand, if I discuss in court about your cross dressing and your sexual problem, this may damage your character. If I discuss what you told me about being arrested when you were nineteen for sex with a minor it would damage your case, I'm trying to protect you Ivan, the prosecution would have a field day with that, they would twist it and make you look guilty"

Ivan understood, he had forgot about the incident with Tasha, she was fifteen, they were in a relationship, but her parents and the police didn't see it like that. He was never charged but he agreed it wouldn't look good if it was brought up now.

Tanya recognising that the cogs of his mind were turning, she knew that she had got him, and got him thinking.

"So you see Ivan, as much as I would like to help you, I think I'd be helping you more by staying out of court".

"Yes, yes" he agreed you are probably right.

They talked for awhile, about superficial things, the weather, how he was coping and then the bell went. Visiting time was over. She left pleased that she had convinced Ivan that her services would be more of a hindrance than a help.

She hailed a taxi, got her train back feeling more relieved than she had in a long time. If she was called to court even as a character witness, then the risk came that the prosecution would look into her past and use that against her.

Her life was comfortable now, no-one knew her and she didn't want that coming out to haunt her. She didn't want to have all of her life resurrected, and Stephen she couldn't bare for Stephen to find out and even if he wasn't in the court he would be told.

This all could have been a nightmare. She needed to be a little bit more choosey about her clientele in future.

The train arrived in Leicester; she needed a drink, a stiff drink. She took out her mobile and rang Stephen.

"Stephen Roberts" he answered, she loved the way he didn't answer with his title. He was not pretentious at all.

"Hi" she said "fancy a drink?"

"Yes, what now?" he asked.

"Yes please" she said "I've had a helluva day, just need to get drunk"

"Wanna talk about it" he asked.

"No thanks, I don't particularly want to relive it, just need to have some fun that's all.

"No problem, fun you shall have, shall we meet in the usual place?" he asked

"That would be good she said, see you soon" and switched off her phone.

Chapter Twenty-Six

Friday 18th April

The music was pounding just like she liked it; she swivelled her body on the dance floor feeling like a movie star. Cocaine had always made her feel like a movie star, made her feel unique and confident.

When she had a line of coke she was no longer the butch tattooed dyke looking bird that she was, she was sexy, beautiful with an hour glass figure that everyone was now looking at and admiring. She could feel their piercing eyes on her body and thrust her hips even more to tantalise them.

They all wanted her, she imagined, they were desperate to have her, to take her, to run their tongues over her luscious body and caress her pert breasts she dreamed.

Floss as her friends called her knew deep down that she was no looker, she had ruined herself in her punk days by the holes left behind from her lip and eyebrow piercings, and her tattooed arms and back that now made her look grotesque and dirty. She wasn't anything special then, but she at least looked clean.

But on cocaine she could forget all that and imagine she was a super model that everyone wanted to fuck.

Guys wanted to fuck her alright, but that was because they thought she was a dyke and they got a thrill out of thinking they'd converted her. She wasn't though, had never even kissed a girl, and had no interest. The only kiss she'd ever given a girl was a Hartlepool kiss, a quick head butt between the eyes.

She was well known too, notorious for being the hardest girl on the estate; she loved a good fight made her feel better about herself.

At this moment in time, she was flying high, the cocaine working its way around her body, making her feel good, making her feel special.

Floss didn't care about the 'crash' that the cocaine would leave her with for the following couple of days. She could always take something else if it got too bad.

She didn't even care that she'd been told that the substance of her choice would make her heart go faster and that her heart would then make her other organs speed up, wearing them out faster. Her lungs, her kidneys, her bladder, all her organs would be a lot older than she was. She didn't give a toss that it may take twenty years off her life.

"Who wanted to live till they were seventy anyway, when all you could do was sit in a chair and wait to die, who wanted that extra twenty years when you were pissing and shitting yourself" she would say.

Floss didn't have a care in the world, she was a drug addict, any time her self esteem felt low, or she felt depressed or anxious, she would just pump herself with drugs and that would diminish those feelings and make her feel good again.

Her body had no value to her anyway, so any do gooder that tried to tell her what she was putting her body and her mind through she just ignored and got on with the life she wanted to live. It was her life, her body and her mind, so 'fuck off' was all she would say.

She felt that getting wasted was an art and tonight she had decided to make a masterpiece, she was adamant she was gonna get off her trolley.

She had always dabbled with drugs, but she had become dependent on them after her mother died.

She was one of three daughters and had always been the black sheep of the family, the one that rebelled, the one that left school at fourteen and terrorised the streets, she loved the fact that she frightened people.

The one that slept around shagged anything with three legs. She was the one that was always in trouble with the police for shoplifting, fighting or nicking cars.

Whereas her sisters were all goody two shoes, stayed on at college, gone to university, required good jobs, met nice blokes and had perfect children.

Then when she was twenty five her mother fell ill, this was her chance to prove herself, it was cancer and it was terminal.

Floss moved in to take care of her. It had to be down to her as she was the only one of the three without children, and Floss didn't mind, she could make it up to her mum, make up for all the bad things she had done, get in her sisters good books too. Black sheep turned white she had thought.

It hadn't worked out like that though, it had been hard work looking after her mum and as much as Floss had tried to people please her and run to her every whim, her mother had still hated her, she could tell, still brought up her past, never let her live it down.

Her sisters weren't much better, they had even accused her of stealing from her own mother while she was dying and spending their inheritance. She had to live on something for fucks sake, she couldn't make any money while she was playing nursemaid. It didn't help that she had spent the money on drugs, but she had to have some enjoyment, some way to chill out once her mum went to sleep in the evenings.

Her drug use had gradually increased, whilst taking care of her mum and had sky rocketed after she died and after all the hassle her sisters gave her.

She took anything now. Cocaine, pills, crack and had even took heroin to bring her down from the crack when she couldn't get hold of any roofies which was the street name for rohypnol.

She was alone now, no family they didn't want to know her, no friends either really. She was not daft she knew that people only pretended to be her friend because they were scared of her. Better to have her as a friend than as an enemy, and her drug using friends were fair-weathered, they only hung around if they knew she had a fix.

She had managed to keep the house though, the council had said that she could stay in it as it was only two bed roomed. So at least she had a place that she could take men home to.

She had even tried to keep it tidy, had decorated it to her liking and brought some new furniture from a loan she had got from the benefits agency. She had shoplifted a few small items too. It was starting to look different now, more modern, she just needed to get rid of the flowery carpets and lay some wooden floor.

She bopped all over the dance floor, not caring who she knocked or got in the way of, she was on a roll now, she'd got the rhythm and fuck did she feel horny.

Cocaine always made her feel that way, helped her to enjoy sex too, she could go all night, not that the men she took home could and she'd given some serious consideration to taking two or three home at the same time.

It was about midnight when he had approached her, offered to buy her a drink. She shouldn't really drink when she was on coke, but what the hell she had thought, and asked for a Bacardi and coke.

He wasn't the handsomest bloke in the place, but he'd do, she thought as he was kissing her neck and sending a shiver of pleasure down her spine. Cocaine could do that heighten your awareness, heighten the pleasure zones.

It wasn't long before they were rubbing their bodies together, touching and feeling each other's genital areas, groaning and breathing heavy into each other's ears, oblivious that people were watching and disgusted in their behaviour.

People were commenting too "Get a room" and "tart" but they were too engrossed to notice, as far as they were concerned they were the only two people in the room.

Their tongues were passionately playing with each other's tonsils, when the bouncer came up and asked them to leave. They both left laughing no sense of pride, no embarrassment and jumped into a taxi that was waiting outside, telling the driver, that their name was that of his booking.

They couldn't keep their hands off each other in the taxi and the fact that he wore a wedding ring had no consequence to Floss.

They arrived at her house and she dragged him by his tie into the passage way and stripped him of his clothes, noticing with disappointment the wimpy body and small penis that he had, but she was not disappointed for long as he pulled her to the ground, unwrapped and slipped on a condom as she ripped her own clothes off and he shagged her in every position imaginable.

Two hours later he was gone, home to his wife she supposed but she was satisfied and that was all that mattered. She hadn't even known his name she sniggered proud of her immorality, not one bit bothered that she was getting quite a name for herself.

She took out her crack pipe and prepared her fix and smoked it whilst listening to her stereo blaring out the deep tones of Amy Winehouse. Thinking of her next conquest and planning what she would get on her next shoplifting expedition.

It took her a while to acknowledge that someone was at the door, to recognise what the banging was, at first she had thought it was the crack playing with her mind.

Someone was banging on the back door. Who the fuck was this, she thought at this time of night.

"Okay, Okay, I'm coming" she shouted "This better be good!"

If it's fucking Leroy after some crack I'll knock him fucking out.

She staggered to the back door, opened it and stared at her visitor.

"Who the fucks are you?" she asked, and that was all she could remember.

Chapter Twenty- Seven

Monday 21st April

Stephen had been sat on Derek's desk talking to him and John when the call had came through at twelve forty five. Another girl had been found murdered only this time it had sounded messy.

They'd all three jumped out of their seats, grabbed their coats and travelled to the scene together, sat in silence all the way absorbed in their own thoughts.

All had been thinking along the same lines, this would be the third murder of a woman in her own home in a short space of time, what the hell was going on, they'd already banged a man up for the other two, had they got the wrong man or is this a separate incident altogether.

Stephen had taken the driving seat, and he headed for the second time in a month to the Peckleton estate. The weather was dry this time and a small ray of sunshine came through the clouds, but the mood in the car had been dull.

The information that they had was that a thirty three year old girl had been brutally murdered, she had been found by Leroy Johnson a local drug addict and criminal and thankfully he had done the right thing and called it in.

All of them had known of Floss, otherwise known as Fiona Stafford, they had come across her at some time in their police career.

A gabby brawd, Stephen had thought, but didn't deserve to die.

On arriving they had walked into a bloody scene that was just being cleared by forensics, there was furniture toppled over and smashed ornaments scattered over the floor.

Some of the forensic team were measuring the blood splatter on the wall and furniture, while others were laying down plastic sheeting to preserve any evidence, and Owen the pathologist was examining the body.

Stephen was stood watching this drama play out before his eyes when Owen opened the girls hand and took out a familiar card. He laid it flat on his gloved hand and at the same time as Stephen he had read the message:

Stephen, gives every bird a worm, but he does not throw it into the nest

"What the hell...." Stephen said as Owen met his eyes.

"I think someone's trying to tell you something mate" Owen said

Stephen's heart was pounding, this was getting personal now, and what the fuck was going on they'd just locked the killer up for Christ's sake.

"Is this the same killer, do you think? He asked Owen.

"Looks like it might be Stephen, I need to get her to the lab, but as a preliminary guess I would say that this wound didn't kill her.......... this did" and he pointed to a blood drenched pillow lying next to the sofa, that Stephen hadn't noticed.

"And I'd also go as far as to say she has been dead for at least two days, so it could be your Friday night killer" he added.

Stephen had left the scene then, his blood running cold. He had to speak with his boss tell him before someone else did. He found Derek and John and told them to get one of the uniforms to bring them back to the station once they'd finished up here and headed for his car.

'Stephen gives every bird a worm, but he does not throw it into the nest.'

He'd heard that quote before, but couldn't remember where and when and he was sure it didn't say Stephen but couldn't remember who.

What did that mean he thought?

'I help people but don't do it for them' – who have I helped?

His mind was racing as he pulled into the station car park and his heart pulsing when he saw that the place was swarming with press. This time there were three times as many as the last time and TV cameras too.

He pushed his way through ignoring the barrage of questions and made his way up to Michael's office.

His boss was pacing the floor on the phone raising his voice in temper as he gestured Stephen to sit down.

Michael ended his call and said "I've heard Stephen, how the fuck did this happen?"

Stephen couldn't answer just raised his hands in despair. They had messed up, he knew that and there was no point trying to argue or justify his actions. He had made the decision to charge Ivan Springer, so he needed to take full responsibility.

"Well it needs to be sorted Stephen, that was Ivan Stringers lawyer on the phone, he wants him released, and not only that he wants your arse put on a barbeque griddle!" he shouted.

"I'll sort it" Stephen answered politely.

"Good" Michael said voice mellowing now "and when you have done that you need to give those animals out there something to get them off our back. You need to do a press release!"

"Yes sir" Stephen replied and walked out of his office knowing that there was nothing more to be said.

****

Stephen was sat at his desk preparing a press release, it was six o'clock and he'd promised to meet with them at six thirty. He'd wanted to get all the details off his team first, find out exactly what had happened.

His team had been thorough; as soon as they had heard about the murder they had got themselves down to the scene and followed John's instructions.

No-one had put him in charge, this was just how John was, if Stephen wasn't around he had always took the lead and no one ever had argued over that with him. No-one had minded.

They had, had a brief meeting at five fifteen and were all back out on the streets again, interviewing potential witnesses, finding out all they could no matter how small. The overtime bill was going to be huge this month Stephen had thought.

Everyone had been subdued at the meeting. Stephen didn't know if this was because they had most likely locked up the wrong man, or they had read the latest calling card and were angry. This was personal now and was aimed at their boss, they didn't like that, didn't like it when it involved one of their own.

With the exception of Paul that is, he was energised, almost gloating, his head held high like a peacock pruning his feathers.

Stephen had ignored this; he couldn't be bothered with arrogant cops, he couldn't be bothered with anyone come to think of it that stealthily boasted 'I told you so,' he didn't have to say the word's, Stephen knew what he was thinking, and quite frankly at this moment in time couldn't give a shit.

Floss had been to Jason's, Paul had reported back that he had been sent there by John on a hunch to go through the CCTV images of Friday night. She was on CCTV getting down and personal with some bloke and had to be kicked out as it was almost being considered as obscene.

She'd then got in a taxi with this same man whose blurred photograph was now being passed around and investigated to see if they could find out who he was.

Derek and John had taken a statement from Leroy, who had gone to the house sometime around mid-day. He hadn't got an answer and was about to leave when he tried the back door. It was open so he wandered in. He was evasive about why he had went round, but all in the room had agreed that he was, in all probability, on the scrounge for drugs.

He'd found the body, said he hadn't touched anything only the phone when he'd called the fuzz, as he kindly referred to them as.

Vera had knocked on neighbours doors and yet again no-one had heard anything except her immediate neighbour who had said that she had been woken up by what she thought was a thud around two thirty but hadn't took any notice and had gone back to sleep.

The taxi driver had been tracked down and he could not recall a description of either of them just said that he was 'glad to drop them off as they were about having it off in the back of his cab'.

They had all brainstormed ideas, and the one difference in this case was that Floss had been hit over the head with a blunt instrument; they were unsure what this was and were hoping that forensics would be able to put some light on this. The place was in such a mess it was hard to tell.

They all concluded that Floss must have put up a fight, and anyone that had known her would know that she would.

No-one could make neither head nor tail of the calling card, but Vera had volunteered to do some research and see if that would enlighten them.

Now it was time to face the press.

Chapter Twenty-Eight

Stephen stepped out into the cold evening breeze and faced the press all clamouring forward for information like vultures scavenging for bread.

"Is it the same killer, is it a serial killer" someone shouted.

"Does that mean you have locked the wrong man up?" said another

"Is Ivan Springer innocent?"

"What do the police have to say about their mistake?"

"Are our women safe on the streets?"

"How close are you to catching him?"

And so, on and so on.

Stephen had waited until they had all stopped. He was not going to be answering their questions individually. He had a ready prepared speech and that was all that they were getting. He held up his hand and commanded silence, and as Stephen always did, he got it.

"Today, we have been investigating a third murder in this city. All three were single women in their thirties, and all were killed in a similar way.

There is a pattern forming and we do believe that this is the work of one man

On Thursday 3rd April we arrested and charged a man for the murder of Jane Smith and Lizzie

Benton, we are now having an internal investigation to assess whether we did in fact arrest the wrong man for these crimes. If this is the case, this man will be released from Winson Green prison over the next couple of days. However we will still be expecting him to help with our enquiries.

The police are doing all we can to solve these serious and unprovoked attacks. We have several leads to follow up and we are working around the clock and will do so until this crime is solved and the perpetrator is caught.

In the meantime we advise that all women are careful, that they walk home in pairs, that they are vigilant and wary of strangers.

We would like to request that anyone that knows anything that may help the police with their enquiries, that they contact us immediately on 0800 990099, no matter how small and any call will be treated sensitively and confidentially.

You have my personal assurance that this man will be caught!

Thank you"

Stephen turned back into the police station ignoring the stream of questions that followed him.

****

They were all sat in the meeting room waiting for Stephen to appear. It was Thursday 24th April and they'd all been working full out to try and catch this killer.

Stephen had called this meeting to look at what they had got, discuss the recently received pathology report and to plan their next move.

Stephen did not have to command silence when he walked into the room this time. They were already silent, they were tired from days of adrenalin boosted work, frustrated from the dead ends they repeatedly kept coming to, and quickly losing their motivation.

Stephen could feel this, he'd been sensing it for the last two days, and had tried his hardest to keep the momentum going, keep their morale that was slowly dropping down high.

It was getting exceedingly harder and harder as the hours passed.

"Right guys" he announced "let's look at what we have got and lets join forces and work out a plan on how to catch this bastard."

"But before we start, I would like to take this opportunity to thank you all for your hard work it has not gone unnoticed by me or the powers to be upstairs, and what I can tell you is that when it's all over and we have this moron safely locked away, there's a big fat gypsy party for you all with free drinks all night and I've had that from the money man himself."

The whole team cheered, morale rising, Stephen knew this would work, that's why he had gone to the trouble of getting it authorised with Michael, a team with a low morale decreased their chances of finding this, now what they all believed, serial killer.

"Firstly" Stephen said as soon as they had all quietened down.

"Fiona Stafford was suffocated with her own pillow as were the others; however it looks like she put up a fight first. There were traces of skin in her finger nails, which were not her own. Therefore our perpetrator may have scratches on him.

The cells have been sent off for DNA and....."

Before he could finish everyone had groaned, he knew the problem, they were thwarted by the time that this usually took.

"and" Stephen added "the database staff have acted with urgency on this one and have scoured their data base, but they do not have a match"

Another groan.

"The positive of that is that when we get him, there will be no mistakes this time we will have his DNA" he paused.

"The pathologist believes that she was struck over the head with a hammer, we are in the middle of trying to get some clarity on if this was her own hammer, borrowed or if maybe the killer brought it with him.

Owen believes that Fiona had intercourse the night of the attack, there were slight bruises inside the vagina, however this could have been down to rough sex rather than a rape, as there was no other bruising on the body to indicate that she was pinned down, however this does not rule out rape." He heard himself saying for the second time this month.

"No semen this time." Again he paused.

"The toxicology report states that she had cocaine, crack and rohypnol in her system

There was no forced entry again as you know, and a calling card was left" he glanced uncomfortably at Paul as he said this. "We all know what the calling card said and I can still not decipher its meaning. Over to you" he said, handing the floor to his team.

Both Vera and Paul went to speak at the same time. Vera hung back and let Paul go first.

"The reason she was able to fight back sir, maybe because she had a high tolerance for roofies, erm rohypnol sir"

"Why would that be Paul?" Stephen asked.

"People that take crack sir often need to take something to bring them down; the most common drugs that they use are roofies which is the street name for rohypnol, heroin, and diazepam or in some cases cannabis. If Floss had been taking roofies regularly for this purpose, then her tolerance would be stronger than say a non drug user"

"Thanks Paul" Stephen said, never able to understand why drug users used drugs to lift themselves up, then drugs to bring them back down, what was the point in that he thought.

"You may have hit the nail on the head, the perpetrator may not have known that, now Vera what have you got"

"The quote sir, it should read God"

"God?" Stephen asked.

"Yes sir, 'God gives every bird a worm, but he does not throw it into the nest' I found it on the internet"

Everyone sniggered.

"So what's he suggesting" Stephen said absentmindedly losing his cool in front of the team "that I'm God!" he asked.

No-one answered. No one dare.

Paul would have liked to but thought better of it.

Chapter Twenty-Nine

How come you are reading this?

Don't you have other things to do, place's to be, duties to carry out and problems to solve?

Isn't every moment spoken for twice over?

No, you just want to invade my personal world again don't you, judge me, and grow to hate me.

Let me tell you something; you do that to avoid, to avoid looking at your own world and its miseries. While you are looking at me and judging me and despising me you don't have to look at yourself do you?

265

Gut Instinct

Well if you really want to know, I don't feel so good today, things went drastically wrong,

I don't know why it didn't work, the drug that is, maybe because she was overweight, perhaps I should have put more in.

I will have to put more in, in future. I can't risk that happening again, I might have been hurt.

I'm depressed now, don't worry about me though as I have my souvenirs, I have the lipstick stains that I can smell and taste.

I hate violence and I had to use violence I had no choice, she fought me like an alley cat, scratched my face, there was a hammer laying on the table so I had to hit her with it.

This is not my style but I had no choice, I hope you can see that.

I hope you don't see me as a monster.

I am not a monster; I just had to protect myself and my identity to enable me to continue my work.

You can see that can't you?

I have victim empathy, I never hurt them, I have only ever suffocated my victims with a pillow.

I learned this method by chance when I was nine years old.

I wanted a pet, but my mother hated animals, she just liked treating people like animals, well me in particular.

One day when she was out I heard a sort of crying at the back door, I wasn't sure what it was but it sounded like something in distress.

I wasn't supposed to open the door to anyone but this day I did.

I found on the doorstep a little kitten, black and white it was. I loved it the minute I saw it and brought it in and gave it some milk.

I wanted to keep it, but she would never let me, would probably hurt it in some way if she saw it.

I worked out a way that I could keep it without her knowing. I would keep it in my bedroom; she would never know because she never went in there.

Gut Instinct

So I did. I even named it, mittens, after its black paws.

I had something of my own, something to love and something that would help me through my miserable days.

I would sneak food up to it every day, and lay newspaper down so that it could do its business and sneak it out to the bin whenever she went out.

My life felt better then, I so loved that kitten.

Mittens had been living in my room for about three weeks when I think I must have given it something that upset its stomach, because one particular night she began crying. I tried everything to console it, but it would not stop crying.

If my mother found it we were both for the chop, so I took it into my arms and took it to bed with me. It still continued to cry.

I put the pillow over its face and after a while it stopped.

I miss mittens with all my heart.

I despised her more after this.

The abuse continued for all of my life, and the sexual abuse was periodic but got more frequent when she didn't have a man to satisfy her.

I began to despise my penis more too, now that she was using it.

I left home just after my sixteenth birthday,

I had made that decision at a very young age. I didn't know where I would go or what I would do, but anything would be better than staying with her.

By this time she had almost stopped going out, she went out to collect her benefits and alcohol and a meagre amount of food once a week and that was it.

She would then sit in the chair all day, she never washed, never changed her clothes and never did anything but watch television and drink.

I was doing everything for her. I had become her slave.

Gut Instinct

She was a full blown alcoholic by this time, her first drink in the morning would be Gin and she would drink through the day rather than eat.

She was deteriorating rapidly and I was not going to be looking after her when she became really ill. She could rot in hell for all I care.

So one morning having packed what little belongings that I had, and stealing fifty pounds from her purse, I left my luggage in the hallway and I went into the now smelly living room and said,

"Mother, why do you hate me so much?"

She looked at me for a long time, almost as if she had trouble comprehending what I had said, then replied,

"I don't hate you son, I just love me more"

"Then why have you hurt me so much?" I asked,

That was it, her usual tirade of abuse came flooding out,

"Fucking hurt you, what the fuck do you think you did to me when I gave birth to you, how hurt do you think I am, that I was given such a useless lump for a son.

How fucking hurt do you think I feel that you have lost me any opportunity I could have had with a bloke.

How fucking hurt do you think I am that I am sat here day after day, lonely with just a deformed idiot to pass my days with.

How fucking hurt do you......................"

At that point I turned, picked up my bags and left never to hear her voice again, never to see her face again.

I left the only home I had ever known, the home that was my prison for sixteen miserable years...........
but not without its eradication, not without doing the one thing that I had always wanted to do.

I eliminated her from my life in just the way she deserved.

Gut Instinct

Ashes to ashes, dust to dust.

My second elimination was my penis.

Chapter Thirty

Tuesday 29th April

Paul was stinking mad again; he had been humiliated and undermined once again by his boss.

Stephen had called a briefing at two o'clock today.

They had discussed the murders and any leads to date which were very few. The murders had been on a fortnightly basis, therefore the consensus in the homicide division was that he would strike again this Friday, and that his victim would almost certainly be at Jason's.

So Stephen had told them all to cancel any plans they had for Friday night as they were going undercover.

About time Paul had thought, he'd been going down there undercover off his own back anyway and had been since the second murder, unbeknown to them lot.

There had been nothing notable, however he had given things some thought and recognised that he hadn't known on these occasions what he had been looking for and neither did they, so Paul had asked if he should put together a profile of what the killer might look like, so that they had some idea what they might be on the lookout for. Well he should have known fucking better! Stephen had retorted:

"No thanks Paul, the team will manage on their gut instincts like they've been trained to do. If I needed a criminal profiler I would have acquired one externally, with far more experience than you have, so just get your glad rags on, on Friday and learn from this team how we do things around here"

That was it, put in his place and subject closed, and that wasn't the worst. Stephen couldn't go obviously because there is a chance that the perpetrator knows him, given the message he left at the last scene, so the imbecile Roberts has put John flipping Waterstone in charge, who couldn't organise a piss up in a brewery.

This was going to be chaos he just knew it, felt it in **his** gut and in his head.

So, instead of getting mad, he had a plan. He was not going to roll a joint tonight, he needed to stay focused.

These murders were happening at an unbelievable frequency, they had left the community on edge, and someone had to do something and the only one that could was him he felt.

"I will do a criminal profile in my own time and at least one of us will know what we might be looking for" he'd decided and so he sat down with a pad and pen and made a start.

Okay he thought what do I know about serial killers, he knew that:

Most of them were organized and nonsocial. Most of them also follow some other basic patterns.

More than 80 percent of serial killers are male, Caucasian and in their 20s or 30s.

They are generally intelligent, and they usually kill Caucasian women. There's no way to "tell" a serial killer simply by his appearance -- most of them look like everyone else.

Often, serial killers exhibited three behaviors in childhood: bed-wetting, arson and cruelty to animals. They are also likely to have come from broken homes and been abused or neglected.

Although some are shy and introverted, others are gregarious and outgoing but actually feel very isolated.

Many theorists point to the troubled childhoods of serial killers as a possible reason for their actions.

He began swiftly jotting down all the information they had on the girls that had been murdered:

Jane   Lizzie   Floss

All had been to Jason's

All single - Two were single parents

All in their 30's

All spiked with date rape drug

All suffocated with their own pillow

No DNA

No forced entry

No trace evidence left of Rohanol

277

So what did this lead him to hypothesize? He began to build a profile, matching the information they had with a serial killers pattern which he wrote in bold. Underlining what he felt was the most probable of the facts.

The perpetrator frequented this **nightclub** often. Did he have some sort of a grudge with the nightclub or was he just an <u>opportunist, knew the type of girl that frequented the place.</u>

Serial killers seek out their victim, by focusing on those venues he is most likely to find the type of person he has chosen to prey on.

He didn't like **single parents**, so maybe he was an estranged partner of a single parent didn't see his kids or <u>he was the child of a single mother who abused him in some way.</u>

The killer's thought process when looking for his victim involved looking around for someone on who to lay the blame for his/her anger and hatred.

He may have been mentally fighting a dominant woman in his life, perhaps his mother. Theorists maintained that most serial killers had experienced emotional problems in their own childhoods.

All the girls were spiked with a date rape drug however none of them appeared to have been raped. Vera was probably right on that one <u>he didn't feel that he could overpower them</u>. So he is possibly slight in build.

However this guy had <u>no sexual motivation</u> at all in his crimes, this was unusual, there was generally some form of sex act performed even if it was to cut the sexual areas of the body. The girls were fully clothed, so no sexual curiosity either.

Could have an <u>insight into police procedures</u> and know that if the girl put up a struggle then there could be DNA in her fingernails. He'd met his match with Floss though and she had put up a fight, he possibly hadn't expected this.

All **suffocated with a pillow**, <u>didn't need to carry a weapon</u> with him, most homes have a pillow, was this just in case he was caught before he killed them, perhaps.

None of them were violent crimes, which was atypical in itself. (with the exception again of Floss, but this may have been due to the Rohypnol not having the usual effect).

Most serial killers were violent and characteristically they would get more adventurous, more violent at each occurrence, they would get more courageous too, making mistakes, this was how they usually got caught.

These had all been soft murders, gentle murders, someone effeminate perhaps. <u>A girl/A woman</u>?

There were exceptions to the rule he thought.

There had been female serial killers, serial killers who began murdering during childhood.

There was no forced entry on all the scenes. The women knew him or her, the women trusted him or her. Most women will let a woman in late at night but not a man?

Most serial killers once they have identified their victim-to-be, then try to win his/her confidence.

He underlined all the main points that he had hunches about, and racked his brain for more information on the sequence of serial killers behaviour. Then he remembered:

The moment of actually causing the victims death, is normally the emotional high for most confessed serial killers.

The serial killer's feeling of triumph normally fades rapidly once the victim is dead, so to prolong his/her pleasure, he/she will often remove and take a souvenir or totem associated with the victim.

No evidence so far of him taking a souvenir, he thought. This was the only thing that struck him as odd and that threw him off course. Most of the serial killers that he had read about took some sort of souvenir.

He moved on to to look at the rest of the evidence:

All were left messages:

Jane: "Guess who?"

Lizzie: "Another one bites the dust!"

Floss: "Stephen, gives every bird a worm, but he does not throw it into the nest"

Now that last one is interesting, it is Stephen he is taunting.

First thing in the morning he made a note to himself to ask Vera, who had already been allocated the job of looking up all the arrests that Stephen had made over the years, for her list and see if any of them match his profile.

Stephen gives every bird a worm, but does not throw it into the nest, he repeated what the bloody hell does that mean?

He hadn't got a clue. He then started to look at building a profile with the limited material that he had.

The perpetrator is:

Someone who visited Jason's regularly
Was a child of an abusive single mother,
Was slight in build
Was not sexually motivated by the crimes,
Didn't like violence
Possibly effeminate – A girl or woman?
Possibly knew the ins and outs of police investigative work.
Knew the girls or was someone they could trust.

Something was missing, something did not add up, he went into the kitchen to make himself a cup of tea and then he had the brainwave, the revelation, the CUPS!

He kept the cups or glasses that he spiked; they belonged to each of the girls, that's why they couldn't find them.

"I'm clever" he boasted "Far too clever for them"

And that's not all he mused.

After a killer causes a death, 'post-homicidal depression' sets in and triggers the cycle of steps to beginning all over again.

This is why a serial killer kills more than once and isn't known to stop killing until he/she is caught or dies.

And I am going to be the one to catch him.

Then we will see the look on Stephen Roberts face! He gloated.

Chapter Thirty-One

Friday 02nd May

Sophie was getting ready in her bedroom, she was not looking forward to this night out, 'Jason's" was not her usual haunt but she had promised to go for her younger Sister Victoria's birthday night out.

It always dumbfounded her how differently their lives had turned out.

There was two years between them; a lot of people would mistake them for identical twins, although that was where the similarities ended.

Victoria was a party girl, had just as many opportunities as Sophie had and yet she had chose to work as a checkout girl and live in that grubby little run down cottage rented on that terrible estate.

Their middle class parents were astounded too; they couldn't understand why she'd dropped out of college and chose 'such a dismal life' as they called it.

Sophie on the other hand had done really well. She was an investment lawyer and lived in a pristine minimalistic furnished apartment in an affluent area of Leicester.

She looked around her bedroom now and thought how she would rather lay on her Japanese style bed, snuggled up with a good book, going to sleep looking out of the floor to ceiling windows at the night stars.

Her boyfriend Kyle was in Paris this weekend on business, so this would be a time when she could have had some 'me' time, instead she'd let her sister talk her into this, what she knew would be an unbearable night out.

Victoria's friends were not exactly Sophie's cup of tea, getting drunk, getting laid or getting into a fight at the end of the night was their idea of a good night out and the worst thing was she couldn't make her excuses and leave early because she'd promised to stay at her sisters so that they could spend her birthday together, shopping and having a giggle like they did as teenagers.

She looked in the mirror at her reflection and said "you'll do", donned her coat and got a cab to meet at one of her sisters favourite restaurants for a bite to eat before they headed off to the club.

****

Seven members of the team were all collected in the main office by seven o'clock as requested. Only Vera missing Stephen thought as he entered the office.

Just as if by magic, she tottered into the room on four inch stilettos to a barrage of wolf whistles.

"Okay, Okay" Stephen interrupted "this is not a stag and hen party. You all need to have your wits about you tonight"

They all quietened down as they always did when Stephen spoke.

"Right" he said "does everyone know what they are doing?"

A unanimous "yes" chorused around the room.

"Then go get him, I don't care if you end up arresting fifty men tonight, as long as we get the right one amongst them. If he looks suspicious watch him, if he smiles at you watch him, if he's hovering and looking at women watch him, if you have any hunches watch him! I want this bastard caught, and I want him caught tonight, is that clear?"

Another chorus of "Yes's"

"Remember to pay particular attention to Caucasian males aged between twenty and thirty. That is the classic profile of a serial killer" he said, avoiding all eye contact with Paul.

"There will be uniformed police in the vicinity" he added, "anyone that you think should be pulled in; give a description on your ear pieces, and the boys in blue will pull them on their way out, they have their instructions and will find something to pull them on." He paused.

"Any questions?"

There was no response; everyone was psyched up to go.

"Paul" he directed his conversation to Paul "I need you to stick alongside Vera all night, don't lose sight of her, she's a woman and therefore a potential target, is that clear"

"Yes sir" Paul responded although his face clearly revealed his displeasure at what he perceived was babysitting duties.

"Okay off you go and good luck" Stephen said ignoring Paul's dismay.

They all left the building, all looking the part for a hopefully good night out at Jason's.

****

There were eight of them snuggled around the table, four bottles of wine already emptied and replaced by four more and that was before the food had arrived.

This was going to be a long night Sophie had thought, as the food was eventually served. They had ordered a mixture of finger food that they could all dip into, barbeque ribs, chicken dippers and sauces, king prawns in batter and mini filled jacket potatoes. It looked delicious.

Victoria was on top form and centre of attention which was how she liked it.

"I don't like these crunchy bits that they've put in the ribs" Sally, Victoria's best friend commented.

"I was thinking that" said another.

"Nor me, they don't usually put them in, what are they" said another chewing on something in her mouth, that seemed to take forever.

"Bloody hell" Victoria exclaimed, looking at her hands.

"What's up now" Sophie asked exasperated.

"My nails" Victoria said "they've all fallen off!"

To which, everyone looked from the bowl of ribs, to Victoria's nails to the contents in their own mouths.

Sophie was the first to realise what had happened, Victoria's nails had fallen into the bowl of ribs and everyone was eating them. She burst into fits of laughter, followed by everyone else.

Perhaps it was going to be a good night after all, she considered.

The meal over with they all got in to taxi's to head for Jason's, Victoria had managed to get VIP passes so they didn't have to queue, which was a blessing as the queue was long that night.

Sophie was surprised with there being a serial killer on the loose, and rumour had it that all the girls had been to Jason's on the night they were killed, and yet it had created a bigger crowd not a smaller one. Some people were just ghoulish she thought or on a death wish.

She'd tried to talk Victoria into them all going to a different venue but she wouldn't hear of it, said that she was not going to be scared off by some lunatic, so Sophie had decided to keep relatively sober so that she could keep an eye on her sister if nothing else it was one good reason she needed to be down this dump tonight.

It was ten o'clock and already Victoria was drunk and chatting to some undesirable bloke, Sophie thought. She had no sense that girl, tonight of all nights and here of all places. She headed in her direction hoping to drag her away.

"Come on Vic, time for a dance with your sister" she said.

"In a bit Soph I'm just talking" she replied annoyed at her rudeness when she was just about to pull.

"No, now Vic" Sophie said protectively, although Victoria didn't see it that way.

She pushed her sister aside and said "Back off Sophie."

Sophie backed away knowing that her sister could get quite nasty in drink, but kept a close eye on her.

Whether she liked it or not, she was not going to let Victoria go off with any bloke tonight, not with things being so unsafe at the moment.

Besides their parents would never forgive her if she let anything happen to her.

Sophie ordered a Pepsi from the bar and watched her sister like a hawk annoyed at her naivety and the fact that she would have to stay here to the bitter end babysitting her.

Chapter Thirty-Two

Stephen was sat in his car, parked up at the side of the road; he was too agitated to go home, he had felt a cloud of depression fall over him and had no idea what it might be. He felt a sense of pending doom and had heard from somewhere that this happened just before a heart attack, that and a need to go to the toilet.

He had received a print out of the backgrounds on all his staff earlier today and this had left him feeling shocked. He had requested this a week or so ago after seeing Paul down Jason's, he couldn't be seen to be singling out Paul, so had requested background information for them all.

There was suspicion that Paul as a teenager had been involved in petty crime, but the police could never get enough evidence together to make an arrest or press charges, his name had come up repeatedly in other investigations.

However what had shocked him the most was Vera's past, although nothing criminal she had experienced a difficult childhood, and some of her relatives had been quite dodgy.

That was his motive for putting Paul and Vera together tonight, so neither of them would go off on their own.

He had been tempted to park somewhere outside the club to keep an eye on them both but it was too risky, if he was seen by them or the killer, if it wasn't anything to do with them it could blow the whole operation.

Stephen had been feeling that it was an inside job for some while now, he couldn't fathom out any other reason for the killer to be taunting him. The killer knew him and was trying to hurt him in some way.

He knew Paul's feelings towards him were negative and he had also noticed Vera's face on the night they were at Bill's party when he had made a joke about Paul.

Also Vera had took the scent off the killer being a woman saying that a woman would not carry a date rape drug, could she be their killer. A woman would let her in late at night, a female police officer.

God, he thought I'm getting paranoid, suspecting my own team members.

He had gone through every arrest he had made over the years in the police force and had come up with nothing substantial and nothing that he felt would lead someone to taunt him.

He couldn't help thinking that this murder spree was 'pay back' to him, he just couldn't work out why and he wished he could remember where he had seen or heard that quote before.

"God gives every bird a worm, but he does not throw it into the nest"

He knew he had, felt sure that he had seen it written on something but could not for the life of him think where. If he could then this might lead to a suspect, or some intelligence on who this killer might be.

"God gives every bird a worm, but he does not throw it into the nest" he repeated.

It was there, he knew it was lying in his unconscious, but couldn't raise it up.

He started his car engine and began to move back into the traffic, still trying to rack his brains.

****

Paul was scouring the room, still feeling resentful that he was put on babysitting duties of Vera when he saw something, something very strange indeed.

It had taken him a while to recognise this person with the wig and the uncharacteristic clothes.

There was something about the suspect that he recognised, something familiar, and then it had hit him like a ton of bricks.

"What the hell!" he thought, and chewed over, what he could remember about his profile of the murderer.

It could be a match he thought.

Then he saw the scratch, about six inches long down the side of his suspects smooth cheek.

"Well, I'll be fucking damned" he said out loud forgetting that Vera was in earshot.

"What?" Vera asked trying to match her vision with Paul's vision to see what he was looking at.

"Nothing" he replied "just someone I thought I knew"

That had got to be more than a coincidence he thought, and everything else could match his profile.

Fuck, fuck, fuck he thought, if he was right this would be a bloody mess, it would also be karma in a big way.

Paul saw no point in telling the others, they would think he was mad, lost the plot or revengeful. He knew where their loyalty lay and that in itself would affect their judgment.

He would just hover and watch, but he was not taking any risks, he was not letting this suspect out of his sight.

And he didn't, trying not to alert Vera he kept his suspect under surveillance for the rest of the night.

He didn't even consider anyone else in the room, and at one point grabbed Vera for a pretend snog when he thought that the perpetrator was looking in his direction.

Vera wondered what the hell he was playing at and thought that he was coming on to her, but he had to keep up the pretence because...............

He had a hunch and he was following it.

Chapter Thirty-Three

Sophie pushed Victoria into the taxi cab, before she could kiss anymore strangers goodnight and tell them that she loved them.

She was horrendously drunk, semi unconscious and weighed a ton. But she was thankful that the night was over and that she could keep her wayward sister safe, for tonight at least.

She'd had to prevent her from going off with different blokes to 'parties' where there would be plenty more booze they had said. It had been a nightmare evening and Sophie would be glad to get home.

Sophie decided that she would talk to Victoria tomorrow over coffee about how concerned she was at how much she put herself at risk. There was no point talking to her now, not while she was drunk.

****

Paul managed to lose Vera; he made the excuse that he was going to the toilet and slipped away, keeping a close eye on his suspect.

He knew that if he had got this wrong he was in big trouble, he'd possibly be up on a disciplinary and there is no way he could say what he thought and why he'd left his team and not communicated with anyone. But he knew he was right, there were too many coincidences, he couldn't be wrong.

The anxiety still chewed away at him, no matter how many times that he tried to convince himself that he was right, his hunches were spot on; there was still this wrench in his stomach that he might be wrong and if he was, he was going to be in big trouble.

He saw his suspect leave the building and he hesitated, what if he was wrong?

Then with minutes already lost, he thought 'fuck it, if I'm wrong then maybe this isn't the right job for me anyway. If I'm wrong than I'll resign', and he dashed out of the club in pursuit of his suspect, leaving Vera to fend for herself.

****

"Do you come here often love?" Vera sidled up to John, who was standing at the bar.

"Only in the mating season" he replied and they both laughed.

"Where's Paul?" he asked concerned that she was on her own.

"Don't know he went to the loo and then disappeared, so thought I'd come and look for a real man to take care of me" she laughed.

"He's probably outside having a spliff" Derek interrupted having walked up and overheard their conversation.

"What Paul smokes dope?" Vera asked.

"It's pretty bloody obvious don't you think" Derek answered, "anyway the nights almost over, you two spot anything?"

"No not really, gave a few descriptions to the boys in blue, like you and the others, but can't say I'm overly convinced we've got the right man" John answered feeling disappointed in the night. "Come on let's call it a night, not a lot we can do now and I don't know about anyone else but I'm whacked."

John gave the nod to the other detectives and then left the club with Vera, hanging on to his arm.

"These bloody shoes are killing me" she said.

Gut Instinct

****

Sophie had managed to get her sister into the house and up the stairs to bed,

"I...Love you sis" she slurred, as Sophie put the bed covers over her still fully clothed body.

"You too" she said but Victoria was completely out of it as soon as her head had hit the pillow.

She turned off the light and went downstairs to make her bed up on the sofa.

****

Paul had followed his suspect by car for twenty minutes, when the car that he was in pursuit of, pulled up outside a dingy cottage on the outskirts of a council estate.

He watched as its occupant sat for a while and then got out and knocked on the door of the cottage. Whoever answered the door spoke for a while and then let his suspect in.

His heart was pounding as he got out of his car and snuck around the back of the building.

The bushes surrounding the cottage were high and he had to climb up and over them cutting his legs in the process from the prickly twigs.

Once over the hedge there was a tree in the garden he was able to hide behind which gave him a reasonably good view of the kitchen diner, through its patio doors.

Both his suspect and a pretty looking woman in her early thirties were sat at the kitchen table, the woman having just brought two cups to the table, and a teapot which she began pouring from.

His suspect and the woman appeared to know each other, and the woman appeared to be consoling his potential predator.

His anxiety returned, his heart was thumping, and his stomach was churning.

'What if I've got this wrong,' he thought 'I have left Vera in potential danger, and abandoned the operation, I will be slaughtered for this.'

He watched the woman get up from the table and walk out of his view, but as she did this his suspect leaned over and tampered with the woman's teacup.

Pauls mind was working overtime was this innocent or was the woman's drink being spiked. He was too far away to be able to see for certain and it was too risky to attempt to move further up the garden.

He watched as the two people sat drinking their tea, it appeared like an innocent interaction between two people late at night, and seemed to go on ceaselessly, although perhaps only minutes ticked by. Paul didn't know he had no sense of time just fear.

Fear that he may have got it all wrong and the trouble he would be in, combined with the fear that he might have got it right and that he was in an impending dangerous situation on his own with no back up.

The woman then got up; she appeared to be wobbling from head to foot as she put her hand to her head.

The suspect stood up too as the woman began to stagger out of view. The suspect moved forward quick, as if the woman had perhaps stumbled and the suspect was going to catch her.

That was it; they were both out of Pauls view.

He waited to see if they came back into view, he waited for what seemed like an eternity, nothing!

He needed to do it now; he needed to make a decision to intervene because if this was not an innocent transaction between two friends late at night he could be too late.

Decision made, his adrenalin was off the scale now and the hairs on the back of his head were stood up. Now or never he thought.

Paul ran like a battering ram towards the patio doors and smashed through them, luckily they were wooden and the wood was relatively old, they splintered and broke quite easily.

He landed on the floor of the kitchen, dazed, then having a clear view to the living room he met his suspect's eyes just as she was putting the pillow over the woman's face.

Paul jumped to his feet, quickly removing his cuffs from his belt ran towards her and managed to grab both her arms and cuff them before she had time to think.

As he did this a small card fell to the floor, the writing face up:

He, who laughs last, laughs longest!

"Tanya Wright I am arresting you for the murders of Jane Smith, Lizzie Benton and Fiona Stafford anything you say will be taken down in evidence and..."

"What the fuck is going on here and who are you?"

Victoria had woken up, came down the stairs and walked into the chaos that was evolving in her living room, with her sister laying on the floor groaning as she was coming out of unconsciousness.

Chapter Thirty-Four

Saturday 3rd May

The homicide room was buzzing, it was seven thirty and all the staff had been notified of Paul's arrest in the early hours of the morning, although not who it was.

Curiosity taking a hold of them they had all gone in early to learn who it was that had impacted on their weekends over the last couple of months and all wanting a glimpse of a serial killer that they had mercifully never encountered before in their careers.

All except Stephen, it appeared that he was not as excited as the rest of them. Rumour went round the team that he was probably pissed off that it was Paul that had made the capture; it was common knowledge between them that Paul was not exactly Stephens favourite amongst them.

They were all astounded when they learned that the killer they had been chasing for the last couple of months was Stephen's girlfriend, and all were making assumptions on how he might react. As much as they had been eager to learn who the perpetrator was, they were even more keyed up at seeing Stephens face when he learned this information.

Paul of course was getting plenty of pats on the back and congratulations from his team and his superiors, he was so glad this had turned out the way it had, and was fully aware of the repercussions if it hadn't. He still had to have his meeting and explain why he had left his team and dealt with this alone, but he was sure they would understand once he explained things.

It was eight thirty when Stephen had arrived, shoulders back, head high and a huge grin on his face, anticipating the praise that he was sure to get for this excellent piece of police work that he had been the lead in.

****

Stephen had walked through the main room and was surprised at the lack of excitement in the main office, he was not a stupid man, he noticed straight away that some members of his team were unable to give him eye contact, and others nodded then looked away.

'What the hell is going on here' he thought as he then noticed Michael stood in his office doorway.

In the seconds it took for him to walk to his door, greet Michael, sit at his desk and watch

Michael close his door, a number of thoughts ran through his head. He couldn't quite fathom out what this was all about, but he knew one thing for sure something had gone drastically wrong!

Michael sat in the chair opposite Stephen and took a deep breath.

"Stephen" he said obviously struggling with what he was about to say. "This is not easy, but I'm just going to get straight to the point"

Stephen's heart was pounding now, he almost felt the urge to cry because he knew, sensed that what he was going to hear was something he wasn't going to like.

"Stephen" Michael said again almost as an avoidance of breaking this awful news to his colleague and friend.

"The serial killer was caught last night as you know, what you don't know is that it was Tanya, Tanya Wright"

It took several seconds for the information to sink in but when it did Stephen's anger was visible.

"That is the most preposterous thing I have ever heard, so is that it, that arsehole has arrested the wrong person," he stood up and banged his fist on the table "my fucking girlfriend, where is she, and where is he? He'll be disciplined for this"

He stopped suddenly noticing Michael's face, he believes this crap, he thought. Michael thinks that Tanya is the serial killer, he felt like he was living in a parallel universe, or on candid camera.

"Surely you......."

"Stephen" Michael interrupted aware of his colleague's feelings. "Sit down" to which Stephen did as he was told.

"Stephen" he repeated "Tanya was arrested red handed attempting to kill another girl. She had another message in her hand at the time of the arrest. The lads have been early this morning to her flat and they have found the card that the messages were sent on with identical matches cut out to the cards we have, they have found personal information about these girls addresses, ages, marital status etc and plenty of names and addresses that may have been her future victims" He paused watching Stephen age twenty years in five minutes. He continued.

"We found 'cups' belonging to the murdered girls that are at the lab now looking for traces of evidence and we are awaiting DNA results to match to the cells found in Fiona's finger nails, but even without those we have enough evidence to charge her."

Stephens head dropped to his desk, Michael aware that eyes were all on him through the glass panes to his office; he walked to the internal windows and shut the vertical blinds.

"When can I see her" Stephen asked.

"Not a good idea Stephen" Michael replied.

"I have to see her Michael, to get some closure"

Michael understood, thought about it for a minute or so and then said.

"You can't see her now Stephen you know that. She is still being questioned and has not yet been charged, we cannot have this case jeopardised."

"I know that but....."

"Let me finish Stephen. Once she has been charged and is ready to be transferred you can have ten minutes with her max. Both John and I will be watching through the three way, and if there is any sign of aggression Stephen we will be in to pull you out, have you got that?"

"Sir" Stephen saluted.

"Right, naturally you are off the case, I have put John in charge and he has instructed Derek and Paul to do the interviewing......."

"But...... Paul?" Stephen asked.

"Stephen you are off the case" Michael replied "Go get some fresh air, a cup of coffee, clear your head and be back here for four thirty, I am hoping it will be all cleared up by then. Okay"

"Okay" Stephen replied.

Stephen grabbed his coat and left the office conscious that all eyes were on him. He never said a word and they never spoke to him.

****

Derek was visibly shaking when he came into the main office after interviewing Tanya Wright with Paul.

"She's a fecking freak" he said grabbing everyone's attention. "One minute she was talking to us normally and telling us how she got the women to let her in the house, by playing on their empathy, saying she had been chased and needed help. The next minute she went into a trance like state and mimicked me all through the interview, my body language and everything I said. It was weird"

"Echopraxia" Paul said.

They all looked at him dismayed, he laughed.

"Sometimes catatonic schizophrenics mimic body movements of others or obsessively repeat what others say. These features are known as echopraxia" he said, feeling chuffed with himself that he had listened in his classes and internalized his learning.

"So what you saying now Paul, that she's a fucking schizophrenic" John asked.

"I'm not a psychiatrist John I can't make that diagnosis, I'm just telling you what I know."

"She's probably faking it" Vera said entering the room in the middle of the discussion. "After all she is a psychotherapist; she'd know all the symptoms. But forget that look at this!"

Vera had been on the computer all morning digging up as much information as she could on Tanya Wright's background. They all were given copies of the information Vera had.

"Fucking hell" was the first response.

"Jesus" was the second.

"Oh my God" was the third and this went on until all eight of the team had read the details that Vera had collated.

"Who's going to tell the boss this?" Derek asked.

There were no volunteers. Not even Paul, he hadn't liked Stephen and this was in a sense Karma but even he felt that this was more than he deserved.

Tanya Wright had been born a boy!

His birth name was Richard Dobson and he had used that name up until he was 18 years of age where he began to live as a woman. He had a sex change operation when he was twenty two years of age.

Chapter Thirty-Five

Tanya smiled at him as he entered the interview room, the same smile that she always gave him whenever he saw her. A pleased to see him sort of smile, a sensuous smile that always sent a shiver down his spine.

It had the same effect today, but a different type of shiver, a cold shiver leading to a nauseous feeling within the pit of his stomach. He struggled to keep himself together, to hide the tremors in his hands that he just wanted to put around her throat and squeeze the life out of her grotesque face. It incensed him that he had once found this woman to be beautiful, graceful and sexy. She had deceived him, betrayed him in the worst possible way.

"Hi" she said in a fashion that they had just met up in a coffee shop, not in an interview suite where she had just been charged with a triple murder and an attempted murder. She displayed no repentance for what she had put him through, how she had duped him; she didn't even appear to feel any indignity for what she had done to those poor women.

It was just Tanya sat there, Tanya as she had always been.

He pulled the chair out from under the table, squeaking across the floor as he did it. It was the only noise in a deathly silent room. He sat down and just glared at her adamant that she would speak the first words. They looked at each other for what seemed like hours, that uncomfortable silence each hoping the other would break it, him with a face frozen in pain and her eyes with a glazed look, but smiling.

How the fuck can she just sit there smiling he thought, he'd fucked her and she was really a bloke, what did that make him. She'd led him on a wild goose chase, murdered three people and left him inane messages that made no sense. Another man had gone to prison for one of the murders, one of her clients.

"Why?" He said no longer able to sit the silence out, he knew that he was probably being watched from the two way mirror, the thought that they may be interpreting the look as something meaningful between them sickened him to the essence of his soul.

"Why not?" she replied, typical Tanya, gave nothing away.

"You fucking made a fool out of me Tanya, you duped me into believing that you were.............." he couldn't even let the words come out of his mouth, he knew for sure they would pour out with the vomit that he was undyingly trying to keep inside.

"Well, well, well" she laughed "it would not be right would it for a woman to make a fool out of a man?"

Another fucking question, could she never give a straight answer to anything, even now, she owed him that, and she owed him the truth.

"You're going down for a very long time Tanya, a very long time, and every minute you are in there I hope that you fucking rot!"

He was losing it, he didn't want to lose it, he would be pulled out and he didn't want to leave that room until he had some understanding of why she had done this, why him, was he just in the wrong place at the wrong time or was it something personal.

"Roses are red Stephen violets are blue. I'm schizophrenic, and so am I – Oscar Levant"

"What the fuck............. Just rot in hell bitch!"

"You will rot for as long as me" she replied her eyes like steel and her face distorting into anger now "you have lain in the same bed as a transsexual serial killer" she retorted. "You've put your cock inside a man" she laughed now, an evil long drawn out laugh.

He wanted to slap her but instead he stood up and threw his chair across the room. He knew that he was never going to get anything out of her, anything that would make him feel better. He slowly walked towards the door. He knew that if he didn't leave now they would come and order him out and he wouldn't give her the satisfaction.

He had just put his hand on the door knob when she said

"Oh by the way, was I as good a fuck as my mother" he turned confused, but she looked away grinning, satisfied, as he left the room running those final words through his head.

Chapter Thirty-Six

So that is my story.

Could I have done something different with my life?

You might say Yes, but the truth is that no I couldn't, I was meant to be given this mother and I was born to eventually kill.

My fate had been decided as soon as I was in that queue. It was decided when I was given 326, it was decided when 325 fell ill.

Gut Instinct

I believe that my life with my mother was just to prepare me for what I was born to do; it was to toughen me up, to help me to develop a hatred that you need to have burning inside of you to enable you to kill.

I had that hatred, I lived with that hatred from the day she ironed my shirt while it was still on my small body, it intensified each time she abused me, so by the time I was sixteen I was ready.

I was ready to kill.

My time in the institution meant that I had to put my desires on hold but once I was out that's when it started.

I am being charged with three murders but there were many more, they were far afield and no-one linked them to me.

Other men were serving time for their murders, I was clever, I would see them pick up men and go home with them and then when they left I would go in and kill them.

The police would get the DNA from her vagina and these men would be charged with the murder. They never ever got my DNA. Just like with Ivan Springer.

It was only when I met him, knew what he did for a living that I began my work closer to home, the work that I was born to do.

I wanted him to suffer too for what he did to me and so I killed two birds with one stone. That was to be my fifth card:

Kill two birds with one stone

But that was to be my downfall, playing too close to home, and not waiting for the right time.

The psychiatrists will say it is down to the abuse I got as a child, they will be arguing it out in court, one will say I am mad and another will say that I am faking insanity to avoid full responsibility for my crimes, but you and I know the truth don't we?

Don't we?

Was I born to kill, or was I born okay and it was my experiences that led me to kill?

Do I have a faulty gene, or am I the result of years of abuse, nature or nurture?

That will always be the question on everyone's mind; theorists will be arguing that point well after I have left this planet.

Am I insane?

That is something you will never know. I will keep that close to my chest. The state of my sanity will decide my punishment.

Will I stop?

No; I won't stop until I have killed her over and over again. Until I can stop women like her producing, until I can stop promiscuous men impregnating women like that. Then the killing will stop, and then every child will have a chance even if they are born to kill.

Like me.

Epilogue

Stephen sat in the airport lounge; he was just Stephen now, no longer Detective Stephen Roberts.

He had resigned from his post and was on his way to see his Sister who lived in Greece. He had two hours to get drunk before his plane arrived and needed to obliterate the memories of the last few days, few weeks, few months in fact.

He had no choice but to resign, she had humiliated him. He had lost the respect of his team he shuddered at the memory of when it had all come out, the whispers, the laughing behind his back, someone had, had the nerve to say out loud knowing he was in earshot "Where was his gut instinct then, when he was shagging a transsexual serial killer!" They'd all laughed, even Derek and John his most valued men.

He couldn't have stayed on, this would never have been a seven day wonder, and this would have followed his career for the rest of his life.

He ordered his first double whiskey from the airport bar and tried to read the magazine he had just brought at the kiosk, but he couldn't focus, his concentration drifting back to the psychiatric report he'd read of the woman he could have, might have fell in love with.

The psychiatric evaluation was embedded in his mind, word for word and would be something he believed he would never forget, it read:

"Tanya is 31 years of age and has recently been charged with the murder of three women and the attempted murder of another. She has been working for the last ten years as a psychosexual therapist for people with transgender or cross dressing issues.

Tanya was born a boy named Richard Dobson to a single mum. He never knew the identity of his biological father.

His childhood appeared to be one of poverty and he experienced severe physical and emotional abuse from his mother, who died in 1996 in a house fire reported to be arson, but no one was ever arrested or charged with this offence.

Tanya or <u>Richard</u> as his birth certificate and medical records read (and what I will call him for the purpose of this report) was very avoidant when I attempted to discuss this with him.

I must add at this point however, that Richard appeared to move from one personality to another during our sessions. Some conversations he spoke and emulated that of a man and in others a woman.

There are very few medical records for Richard up until the age of sixteen when he was admitted to a psychiatric unit in London after trying to cut off his penis and almost bleeding to death. He spent two years in this institution and was diagnosed at the time of having a multiple personality disorder with sociopath tendencies.

He disclosed to his psychiatrist Dr. Frederic Burns (report attached) that he felt like a man trapped in a woman's body. Dr Burns arranged therapy for him with a transgender psychologist, he engaged extremely well in therapy and he was subsequently discharged aged eighteen reported to be safe to return to the community.

He lived as a woman for four years and during this time went to college and then university to study psychotherapy followed by psychosexual therapy. After three years in training he was working on a placement with a transgender service.

Aged 22 during the summer holidays he flew to Thailand and had a complete gender change operation.

Richard has been living and working as a woman ever since under the name of Tanya Wright.

Richard does not appear to have gotten over the dreadful abuse inflicted by his mother who he describes as promiscuous and callous.

These memories and feelings were resurrected after meeting an ex lover of his mothers Detective Stephen Roberts who ironically worked on the murder investigations.

There had been an incident when he was about seven years old where he had walked into the kitchen wearing no pyjama bottoms, having wet the bed, and his belief is that his mum's lover Detective Roberts had laughed at his penis, which he had already grown to believe was an abnormality, a protuberance that shouldn't be there.

This had caused him extreme distress and had also resulted in his mother hitting him causing a three inch scar still visible today on his forehead and subsequently locking him in an under stairs cupboard on a weekly basis for long periods of time, when she had brought men to the house,

In Richard's disturbed mind the women he killed were comparable to his mother. He believed that he could kill two birds with one stone, kill 'his mother' over and over again and laugh at the man trying to catch him, just like this man (Detective Stephen Roberts) had laughed at him all those years ago.

He believes that his role in society is to save the benefit system from future pay outs to single parents and he also has a magical belief about birth numbers, his own birth number being 326, this indicates to him that he was to kill three single mothers, two single people without children, but of childbearing age and six promiscuous men, fortunately he did not get to carry out all of these murders.

My diagnosis of Richard is that he is a sociopath and demonstrates symptoms indicative of a multiple personality disorder, and narcissistic personality disorder possibly developed due to the severe abuse experienced in childhood.

My view is that he demonstrates Narcissistic traits due to the fact that he sees himself as 'special' to complete the work he believes that he has to do. For example he believes that he helps others by getting rid of 'vermin' (women like his mum) and saving the benefit system using magical beliefs about birth numbers.

On the other hand he also demonstrates traits of multiple personality disorder due to his distinct and separate personalities. He demonstrates an unawareness of each other's existence.

The male persona having quite a violent view of the world and the female persona that has empathy which he has demonstrated in his crimes by suffocating his victims with a pillow, This makes him different from other serial killers – killing people in a kind way.

Sadly he also demonstrates symptoms indicative of schizophrenia.

My professional opinion is that Richard is not and was not of sound mind when committing these crimes"

Stephen felt sick as he ordered his third double whiskey; he had been having sex with a transsexual serial killer for the last 10 months.

How would he ever cope with that, he knew it would crucify him for the rest of his life, leave him with the psychological problems his perpetrator had lived with for most of his life?

He could remember the incident clearly now, his mother was a one night stand, like most of the women in his life at that time, yes he had laughed, laughed at the pyjama top he'd had on and the writing on it:

'God gives every bird a worm, but he does not throw it into the nest"

He'd laughed because of 'the little worm' hanging down limply below this slogan.

If only he had known that this would have such an impact on a child's life.

But he couldn't see this creature as a child now, as much as he tried.

After reading the psychiatric report he knew that she, he would not go to prison, that her barrister would claim insanity, she'd go to a psychiatric institution and charm her way out in two years.

He suddenly stopped mid thought........ That's what she was getting at, in the interview room..........

Gut Instinct

'Roses are red Stephen.......................'

She was trying to tell him that she would fake insanity; she even had the psychiatrist fooled.

She was having the last laugh.

'He, who laughs last, laughs longest.'

****

It was time to go to the boarding lounge now, start a new life in Greece, what he was going to do he had no idea but it would be a fresh start where no-one knew him, no one knew what a mess he'd made of his life.

He boarded the plane and smiled at the air stewardess, she smiled back obviously attracted to his manly looks and dazzling eyes.

Life was going to be good now he thought, he knew it was after all he could feel it in his gut.

Gut Instinct

AUTHORS NOTE

While writing this book, I was just finishing the fifteenth chapter when my husband called me out the office and said "Hey Linda, come and look at this". He had the tele text on, and this is what it said.

"Creativity is often part of a mental illness, with writers particularly susceptible, according to a study of more than a million people.

Writers had a higher risk of anxiety, bi-polar disorders, schizophrenia, unipolar depression and substance misuse, the Swedish researchers at the Karakinska Institute found."

That's why you can get inside the mind of a serial killer he teased.

What a load of rubbish I replied. Because I didn't write this book................... my alter ego did.

I didn't like to remind him that he came home from work every evening asking if I'd wrote the next chapter yet as he wanted to read it, so what did that make him.

I sincerely hope that you enjoyed reading it as much as I enjoyed writing it, and if my husband has me sectioned please come and visit me.

I would like to give a big thank you to the people who have supported this new adventure of my life and for their continuous positive feedback. They include:

Elaine Woolmore, Ann Hirst, Giuliana Davies, Claire Kilmurry, Sheilagh Roxborough & Julia Quinn.

Thank you also to Dr. Baljit Mann for her psychological input and alongside my husband Michael David Mather and my stepson Dr Michael William Mather a big thank you for proof reading my book and for your valued feedback.

Thank you for buying and reading this book. I hope you enjoy.

Exploring your thoughts:

Did you develop any empathy for the killer? – The killer had a horrific childhood did you feel sorry for him.

Do you think that his childhood had a huge impact on his behaviour now? – Is this an excuse for what he did or do you feel it's not surprising how he become as an adult?

Do you think he was born this way or nurtured this way? – Was he born to kill or did his nurturing or lack of it lead him to this.

Were you surprised at who the killer was given the profession that s/he was in? – is it your expectations that people in high professions are not sociopaths.

What do you feel about Stephen's behaviour towards Paul? – Was he jealous or just irritated?

How do you feel Stephen may have felt once he knew who the murder was? – Shame, guilt, embarrassed, humiliated.

Do you think he deserved to feel like that? – He had humiliated Paul and undermined his skills so did he get his comeuppance.

What did you think at the end?

Was the killer faking mental illness? Think about what he said at the end about all the other murders he had committed and not been found and his magical numbers that he told the psychiatrist about.

Did his or her professional skills enable her to fake her symptoms?

And would an experienced psychiatrist fall for it if s/he was faking it?

I hope the book has given you a lot to think about it certainly did me as I was writing it.

Website: www.linda-mather.co.uk

E-Mail: mather_linda@sky.com

Gut Instinct

15395627R00186

Made in the USA
Charleston, SC
01 November 2012